DEATH ON
THE COLLEGE LEVEL

"Oh my God, come quickly! There's someone at the bottom of the pool!"

Glad Gold popped her glasses on as she ran. She slowed down as she stepped onto the slippery tiles at the pool's shallow end. Next to the edge lay a catcher's mitt, a bunch of paper roses, and a bloody baseball bat.

Henderson Neville Knight was fully clothed in his Harris tweed suit. He was lying face down, undulating, below the surface of the water. His arms were bent, his fingers swollen as sausages; his handsome silver hair streamed and swirled out darkly in the water. The back of his head was black with clotted blood.

"Who *is* that?" asked Ms. Day in a horrified whisper.

"That's the president," said Glad. "Somebody finally did it."

KNIGHT MUST FALL

THEODORA WENDER

AVON
PUBLISHERS OF BARD, CAMELOT, DISCUS AND FLARE BOOKS

KNIGHT MUST FALL is an original publication of Avon
Books. This work has never before appeared in book form.
This work is a novel. Any similarity to actual persons or
events is purely coincidental.

AVON BOOKS
A division of
The Hearst Corporation
1790 Broadway
New York, New York 10019

Copyright © 1985 by Dorothea Wender
Published by arrangement with the author
Library of Congress Catalog Card Number: 84-91197
ISBN: 0-380-89520-X

First Avon Printing, February, 1985

AVON TRADEMARK REG. U.S. PAT. OFF. AND IN OTHER
COUNTRIES, MARCA REGISTRADA, HECHO EN U.S.A.

Printed in the U.S.A.

WFH 10 9 8 7 6 5 4 3 2 1

Chapter One

March 14: 11:45 a.m.

"MRS. PEPPER! What's bawling?"

Polly Pepper looked in from her adjoining office. "Pardon me, Mr. Knight?"

Henderson Neville Knight assumed a patient look and repeated his question. "What's bawling, Mrs. Pepper?" he asked.

"I'm sorry, but I don't hear anything," said the motherly Mrs. Pepper, puzzled.

President Knight waved a piece of paper at Mrs. Pepper. Lined paper, with holes in it, designed for a three-ring notebook. On the page: handwriting in brown felt-tip pen. Folded several times, to fit a small white Turnbull College envelope which lay on his desk. "It's a word," he said. "B-A-L-L-I-N-G. I thought you might know what it meant. Having teenagers of your own."

"Oh, no, Mr. Knight, I can't say I've ever heard it. Would you like me to ask Mrs. Angelo? Do you think it might be—you know—naughty?"

Mrs. Angelo was the dean's secretary, and the biggest gossip on campus—except, of course, for the faculty. President Knight shook his handsome head firmly. "Get Amanda Tweedy for me," he said.

"Right away, Mr. Knight."

Mandy Tweedy was the new Dean of Students, still a sixties flower child, but trying to be an eight-

5

ies hot ticket besides. She looked about fifteen years old; yet, on the other hand, she behaved like a woman of, perhaps, sixteen. She had freckles and long red hair, wore Indian cotton skirts or Liz Claiborne jeans, and was part of Turnbull College's new desperate drive to appear With It. Or at least not entirely Out of It. President Knight asked Mandy Tweedy to sit down, then told Mrs. Pepper to close the door behind her.

"This must be absolutely confidential," he said to Mandy, holding the letter in his hand, but not showing it to her.

"Check," said Mandy, flipping her long, shiny hair over her shoulder.

She knew what *balling* meant.

"Fucking," she said.

President Knight couldn't, at the moment, remember what had possessed him to hire Amanda Tweedy. As was his custom when enraged, he chuckled paternally. "Now, Mandy," he said in his kind presidential voice, "don't you think you might choose your language a little more carefully when you're talking to an old gaffer like me? Huh? Even though we all recognize and appreciate how hard you've been working for the College, and what a fine beginning you've made. . . ."

Mandy found his voice as soothing as a massage. Sensory awareness massage was something she was still really Into.

"Thanks, Henderson," she said. "Like, may I ask who's been balling who? Is it . . . I mean . . . something I should know about? You know?"

Balling *whom,* he raged in his mind. These Turnbull alumnae!

He smiled tolerantly. "I think this is one I'd better handle myself."

"Oh," said Mandy, rising. "Faculty? Like, balling with a Turnbull student?"

"Have you heard any rumors?" inquired the president. His face betrayed an unspoken but chronic complaint: Why doesn't anyone ever tell me anything?

"Well, I mean, it happens all the time," laughed Mandy, flipping back a strand of her long red hair.

This was intolerable. President Knight decided to indulge himself. As a warning to Amanda. He raised his resonant voice. "By God, it's not going to happen anymore!" He pounded his fist on the teak desk. He could feel his face reddening under the glorious mop of snowy hair. "Not while I'm president of Turnbull! And you'd better watch out for your job, young lady!"

Mandy crept away, cowed.

But by the time she reached her office at the other end of the corridor, Mandy's cheerfulness had returned, and she asked her secretary, Rowena Jackson, to step in for a moment.

"Hey, shut the door, Rowe," she said excitedly.

Mrs. Jackson, a wonderfully competent and gossipy young black woman, closed the door and sat down. Mandy told all, as she always did with Rowena, who was not only a first-rate assistant, but also her best friend.

"Wow," exclaimed Rowena, "which professor do you suppose has got caught?"

Mandy lit a cigarette, inhaled lustfully, and started speculating. "Old Ferenczi? Bob Bellows?"

"But he doesn't count, surely," objected Rowena. "Bob isn't married."

"True. But maybe, like, his being chaplain might make a difference. You know?"

"Witherspoon?"

Mandy frowned. "I hope not. Dear Jack. He's such an ass about young girls. But it might be. He's certainly been pretty obvious with C.C. Duxbury."

"Oh, I have an idea! Ruy Lopez! I mean, he certainly gets around."

Rowena laughed. "You know what one of the students told me about him?"

Mandy leaned forward. "What? What?"

"He's a really uninspired lover."

"No!"

"Yes. With that sexy accent and all. Real wham bam thank you ma'am. They call him Ruy Blah."

"Ho ho ho! That's great . . . Well, Rowe, ask around. See if you can find out who it is, and who snitched to Knight. I mean, it really won't do to go shocking the president. We really have to protect him from these things."

"Yeah." Rowena went back to her office.

"Mrs. Pepper," called Henderson Knight.

"Yes, Mr. Knight?"

"Please ask Jack Witherspoon to drop in as soon as possible."

The letter was unambiguous, certainly. Now that he understood the mysterious word *balling.*

Dear President:

I'll bet you'd like to know that Proffessor Witherspoon has been balling a Turnbull student, C.C. Duxbury by name. I can tell you more if your interested. Signed, A Concerned Student.

It was almost lunchtime, and President Knight had a busy afternoon facing him. He felt old and tired of academic rigors, and he dreaded most of the day's appointments.

He wasn't old, actually; he was in his middle fifties. But he had been at Turnbull for nine years, and it was time for a change. He knew it, and so did the faculty and students—and the trustees. So it had been a relief to all when he had been offered, and had accepted, a good foundation job. Now he was serving out his time tidying up loose ends, sitting for his portrait on Saturdays, and whittling away at the big budget deficit so that the books wouldn't look too bad when he left. And so that his successor, not he, would be blamed if the economic catastrophe which had been looming over Turnbull for several years finally occurred. He steadfastly refused to make most major decisions: "In all fairness," he said, "that sort of judgment should be left to my successor."

Other decisions, however, he was glad to make—firing certain people who were popular but had always irritated him, refusing to hire a gynecologist for the students, eliminating the Italian department: "In all fairness," he explained, "that sort of judgment should not be left to burden my successor." In the meantime, the search committee (four trustees, three faculty members and two students) were working to find his successor. Six finalists had been chosen, and were coming to the campus, one at a time, to see and be seen by the motley assortment known as the College Community.

It would be a woman, of course, he thought bitterly. Inevitable. Sign of the times. He had given Turnbull his prime years. He had wheedled and strong-armed and conned rich people and foundations into donating four new dorms, a student center, a new library and an Olympic-size pool with underwater lights. Now they were all down on him. The trustees were mad at him because of the deficit. Well, *he* couldn't control the price of oil, could he? He had tried to attract some oil money by starting an Arabic studies department, and the damn faculty, with their childish pro-Semitism, had quashed it.

The students, he supposed, were mad at him because he didn't go into their dorms and smoke pot with them. He always wore a tie and he wouldn't let them turn the place into a brothel. With the infirmary giving out birth control pills! Childish!

The faculty was mad at him for raising buildings rather than their salaries and for paying more to men than to women. Childish! They just didn't understand supply and demand. If you have to offer more to attract a good man, you offer it. Nothing to

do with men being *better*. They just don't come as
cheap as good women. The faculty further complained that he hadn't turned Turnbull into Wellesley.

Well, Turnbull *wasn't* Wellesley—or even
Wheaton. It was a good women's college with a beautiful rural campus and beautiful rich students, and it
would be lucky to survive another ten years, what
with middle-class people not having babies anymore. It was mostly a question of endowment.

Faculty thinks it's easy, mused the president. Just
a matter of attracting more students. Image. Call
the girls "women." Call everybody "Ms." Courses in
pottery and witchcraft. Get Turnbull's name in the
paper, no matter how. Get a woman president. Preferably a black one—in blue jeans. Ha ha.

She'll soon find out. *They'll* soon find out.

The handsome president took vindictive pleasure
in contemplating the faculty's inevitable disillusion-
ment when its longed-for woman turned out incompetent. And *her* bewilderment and sense of betrayal
when they—inevitably—turned on her like the pack
of ill-trained mongrels they were. And the trustees.
Ha! Now those guys were nervous about getting a
woman, of course; at least somebody had good sense.
But the trustees would be even more tight-fisted
with her than they'd been with him; it would be a
real debacle.

Tucking the letter into a desk drawer, Henderson
Neville Knight turned to his appointment calendar
with renewed good cheer.

2:00: Mary Anne Reilly. That would be a sticky
one. Miss Reilly was one of the faculty spinsters, in
her sixties. Once, apparently, a promising astronomer. She had been at Turnbull thirty-some years,
had given everything—her energy, her once-famous
beauty, her whole mind—to teaching. She was beloved on campus, but Knight wasn't sure why; the
woman had a damned waspish tongue.

He was scheduled to tell her, today, that Turn-bull's coffers contained no money for her proposed sabbatical. She wanted to do some observing at Kitt Peak in Arizona, where the air is clear. Something about double stars. But a sabbatical wasn't to be regarded as a reward for past service (as President Knight often pointed out), and Miss Reilly had only three more years before retirement. She would have to forgo the leave. Of course, her pension—with the economy in its present shaky state—might not allow her to go to Arizona. But she could still look at the stars through the campus telescope, couldn't she? Anytime she wanted.

The sabbaticals would be conferred on vigorous young men with books in them. And a few women, of course. There was an occasional ambitious woman on the faculty, like pushy Glad Gold, in English. But generally the women scholars weren't as business-like as the men: They took too long revising, and they kept shifting their areas of interest, instead of just picking a good narrow specialty, getting all the reading done early, and then mining it for all it was worth. The administration had a generous sabbatical policy for young men with books in them because books would enhance the institution's prestige. Books would also get the young men job offers from prestigious coed schools. And some of the vigorous young men, in gratitude for Turnbull's magnanimous sabbatical policy, or perhaps because of the beautiful restful campus and beautiful restless students, might even refuse those flattering offers.

Well, poor Mary Anne Reilly. This was one of the disagreeable tasks in a conscientious president's day.

2:30: *Charlene Christiansen.* That would be another tricky interview. Charlene was the aggressive chairman of physical education and the tennis coach. Fortyish, divorced with a couple of kids, big blonde, surprisingly pretty for a female athlete. She had made the appointment, no doubt, after hearing the rumor that the educational policy committee planned to abolish the gym requirement. And with the requirement gone, of course, most of her department could be fired. A matter of money.

Actually, Knight approved of physical education, was a fine swimmer himself, and was immensely proud of the glamorous new pool Turnbull had just acquired. But he would have to tell Mrs. Christiansen that it was a matter of academic policy, and therefore all in the hands of the ed pol committee. Her colleagues were in charge of curricular matters, he would say. As the chairman of the committee, he only voted when there was a tie.

He wouldn't tell her that he had threatened the committee with the loss of one of their own academic departments if they didn't recommend dropping the gym requirement. "Which would you like to see eliminated?" he had asked. "German? Classics? Physics? Drama? It's entirely in your hands. The faculty, quite rightly, has complete control over the curriculum." Professor Felix Werner of the German department had moved that the gym requirement be eliminated; Professor Mandelbaum (physics) had seconded the motion.

Charlene Christiansen lacked access to the faculty grapevine; she commuted from Plymouth. She might not have heard about that meeting. But she was to her department as a tigress to its cubs; she wouldn't give up easily. And she was a clever parliamentarian. In a faculty meeting the year before, she averted one direct threat to her department by a timely referral to committee. The president rather looked forward to his meeting with Charlene; it was always stimulating to spar with an aroused opponent.

3:00: *Lucille Walker England.* A candidate for his job. The search committee was bringing the finalists in almost every day now. Knight had to see each one and do his spiel on the problems and challenges the position offered. And to look them over. The committee would ask him for an opinion when the last of the group had been seen, but no doubt they'd disregard his opinion when he gave it. Yesterday's candidate, Williams, the token man, had seemed like an all-right sort, well-spoken, tactful, dean of Prentice College, a good Midwestern school. The last one, tomorrow's, looked like a horror from the vita. Diane Day. Only an associate dean, and from Osborne College, a permissive, progressive, far-out place that was about to go under. A writer of poetry and founder of women's caucuses. Two days ago, the second candidate, Shirley Rosen, had been a competent, fast-talking, aggressive dean from one of the big proletarian city universities. Smart. Appalling accent. Not the Turnbull sort.

Today's lady? She was the only one he knew already. As Lucille Walker, she had been a grad student of his at Berkeley, when he was just starting out as an assistant professor. She wouldn't do. Quite smart, though, and not bad-looking, if she'd kept her figure. Wonder where she finally finished her degree? No scholar, but had made it, apparently, as an administrator at Stott College, a rather good women's school in the South. Steady climb: assistant to the dean, registrar, director of admissions, dean of the college, vice president. They must have loved her at Stott. President Knight hadn't seen Lucille Walker England in twenty years and didn't feel much enthusiasm about renewing the acquaintance. Just going through the motions.

3:45: Joe Silva. Head of security. Tell him to fire the campus guard who was caught drunk yesterday. Routine.

4:00: Irma Freundlich. Chairman of political science. The campus crazy. To discuss hiring a replacement for Howard Disher. That would be difficult since Irma's craziness took the familiar, though slightly old-fashioned, form of finding Communists under bushes, and her reaction to every applicant for the job was that she had uncovered another party member seeking to infiltrate the poli sci department. The very fact that the applicant was a graduate of Harvard (Yale, Princeton, Columbia . . .) proved it positively in each case.

Turnbull College was fairly lucky to have only one tenured paranoid schizophrenic on its faculty. Most institutions of comparable size had two or three.

Pity about Howard Disher. He seemed a pleasant young man, always giving parties. Cherubic-looking, with a family to support. But when Irma Freundlich had discovered that he subscribed to the *New York Review of Books*, his days at Turnbull were numbered. Disher hadn't yet found another job, though, and the year of grace was running out. This was his last semester as a teacher.

There was one additional item on the calendar. *7:30: Oceanid Show, "Batter Up."* The annual water ballet, this year with a baseball theme, this year in the marvelous new Pearce Memorial Pool, just across the garden from the president's house. It was always terribly boring, of course, since one can perform only a limited number of maneuvers in the water; but the president's wife, Melanie, was stubbornly fond of Oceanid shows, and there would be no way of avoiding it.

All in all, a rather typical day.

Almost lunchtime. Melanie would be expecting him. But duty came first: Mrs. Pepper announced that Professor Witherspoon was waiting to see him, and that he had a call on line one. "I think it's a student. She wouldn't give her name or say what it's about," said Mrs. Pepper disapprovingly.

"I'll take it," said Knight. "And I'll see Witherspoon as soon as I'm finished with the phone call."

From her desk, Mrs. Pepper tried to eavesdrop, but the soundproofing between the two offices was disappointingly effective. What with Jack Witherspoon sitting right there with anxiety all over his handsome, lined face, she couldn't very well listen at the door. She did, however, catch isolated phrases—"the pool?" and "couldn't possibly" and "so late?"—but the president never revealed the obnoxious student's name. Why did the poor man wear himself out, catering to all these professors and administrators, and even *students?* The man's a saint, thought Mrs. Pepper. That's why.

Chapter Two

March 14: 11:15 p.m.

"SO HE ASKS the madam if there's a girl about six-feet-two and ninety-five pounds," said Glad. "Sort of like me, you know?" Professor Glad Gold, who was five-feet-eleven, was telling the greyhound joke to the red-haired Dean of Students, Mandy Tweedy.

They were partying after the Oceanid Show, at Howard Disher's house on Forsythe Street, abutting the campus. It was one of the cheapie college houses, and much too small for Howard and Barbara and their two kids, but the Dishers were great party-givers. The fact that Howard's contract hadn't been renewed didn't stop them at all.

Widely recognized as the most popular couple on the Turnbull faculty, Howard and Barbara were jolly, fun, smart, kindhearted, energetic and full of public spirit. There was nothing wrong with them—except, perhaps, for a certain slightly unnerving lack of spitefulness. He was an extremely popular teacher, had published respectable, workmanlike monographs on the politics of West Africa, and had labored diligently on behalf of the Black Students' Union (whose members considered him almost an honorary black), the Woman's Action League (which had formally elected him an Honorary Woman), and the Gay Students' Alliance (by whom he had been named an honorary Lesbian).

Barbara Disher was the campus earth mother. With her charm, cuddly sexiness and beautiful, slant-eyed face, she had made fat fashionable in Wading River. She was a tireless feminist, local pol (on the school board), and super-mom—perhaps even more beloved than her husband. She was also one of the roughest players in the regular Wednesday afternoon faculty basketball game.

Mandy stamped her foot. "Will you all shut up! I want to hear the end of this one."

"*So*—the man with the greyhound says she'll do, and takes her upstairs." Glad paused to light a cigarette.

"Still leading the greyhound?"

"Still leading the greyhound. And he asks the girl to get down on all fours. 'Now wait a *minute,*' she says, 'if there's going to be anything kinky I charge double.' 'That's fine,' says the man, 'just get down on all fours.' "

"Can I get anybody a drink?" asked Howard Disher as he brushed past.

"Anyway . . ." said Glad, "she gets down on all fours . . ."

"Oh, the greyhound joke," said Howard.

"And he turns to his dog, points to the girl, and says, 'See? *That's* what you'll look like if you don't eat.' "

"Oh, I'm so relieved," roared Mandy. "Now, Father Bob, what about your college chaplain joke?"

Bob Bellows *was* the college chaplain. Episcopal, but officially nonsectarian. He was young, moviestar handsome, and unmarried. His companion for the evening—a Turnbull senior—stood at his side and smiled. "Well, it won't seem like much after the greyhound joke," he said.

"C'mon, don' 'pologize. Tell it, Bobby," commanded Rachel Witherspoon, waving her drink.

"Well, it's just a saying that some of us in the academic religion game have, about how important it is to write scholarly articles. What we say is, it's either publish or parish.''

Rachel wept with laughter.

"Can I get anybody another drink?" Howard, ever the perfect host, asked again. There were several takers, and after some regrouping Glad Gold (English) found herself talking to Howard (political science), Mary Anne Reilly (astronomy), and Jack Witherspoon (art history).

They were discussing the Oceanid Show, which they all had just attended.

"Face it," Howard expounded, "there are just so many things you can do in the water."

"Everybody puts up her right leg," said Miss Reilly. "Then everybody puts up her *left* leg." (Miss Reilly was 62, had chronic back trouble, and wished all these people would start sitting *down* soon.)

"Then, they all join hands and form a big star," contributed Glad.

"Then everybody puts up the right *arm;* it's really nifty," added Howard.

"Well, at least it's only one hour long," said Jack Witherspoon, with not a trace of a smile crossing his weary, bearded face. He didn't look at all happy. Then again, he never looked happy; that worried tubercular expression was part of his charm.

"And only seems like three," said Mary Anne. "Whatever possessed them to use baseball for a theme this year?"

"Oh, I know the inside story on that," said Glad. "C.C. Duxbury, who's in my Victorian poets, is the president of the Oceanids and also the star shortstop for the Turnbull Bullies. A real jock. So she dreamed up that bit where the girls batted crepe paper roses into the audience before diving into the pool. And she played the part of the comic umpire. A cutie, that's our Cecilia. She's a functional illiterate, though."

"Excuse me," said Jack Witherspoon abruptly, and made his way as rapidly as possible across the crowded living room. He seized his drunken wife by the arm, thanked Barbara Disher for the lovely party—and the Witherspoons were gone. Just like that.

"Ooops," said Mary Anne Reilly.

"Ooops is right," declared Howard. "C.C. Duxbury is Jack's—uh—heartthrob, isn't she?"

"Omigod," said Glad. "I didn't know." She pounded her forehead. "Dumb, dumb, dumb."

"C.C. Duxbury is dumb; I had her in astro intro," said Miss Reilly. (How she ached to deposit her plump body into a nice, hard-backed chair! The crowd was beginning to thin; soon she would be able to ease her sciatica.)

"Hey, Mary Anne, is your disc bothering you?" asked a concerned Glad. "You have that look on your face."

"Why don't I get some chairs from the kitchen?" asked Howard.

"I thought you'd never ask," sighed Mary Anne.

When they were seated, the topic of Jack and C.C. resumed.

"I think he's an idiot," said Mary Anne. "I love Jack dearly—we all do—and there's no question about his being a fine teacher, but what is it that comes over these fourty-five-year-old men, that they put their jobs in jeopardy, and their perfectly reasonable marriages, and run around like absolute ninnies after these silly children? I'd be more understanding if he went for someone like you, Glad."

"So would I," agreed Howard, attempting a leer, but not succeeding. Howard was a real teddy bear, already comfortably middle-aged at 32, with his cuddly teddy bear wife and kids.

"So would I," laughed Glad. "But you know, it's hardly intellectual companionship they're looking for."

"It can't be sex, either," interposed freckled Mandy Tweedy, as she plopped down on the floor beside Miss Reilly. "I mean, like, I'm positive that the average thirty-three-year-old is much better in bed than, like, the average eighteen-year-old."

Glad laughed. "Right on the button! Do you know the month and day, too? And my height and weight?"

"You're a Virgo," said Mandy calmly. "And you're five-feet-eleven, one hundred thirty-five pounds. It's all in the records in the personnel office. Anyway, I mean, what do you think?"

"Five-ten and three-quarters," Glad amended.

"I think it's just to regain their lost youth," said Howard. "It's really hard on men, being teachers, you know. You keep getting older every year, but the students stay the same. They're always eighteen. They're always pretty."

"Not just the men teachers," Glad pointed out. "We're all rather fixated on adolescence; that's one of the reasons we went into this business. But the teacher–student relationship is sort of sexy. And sacred. Like doctors and patients. Or maybe priest-confessor. If the process is working well, the junior partner *should* be in love with the senior."

"And what about the senior partner?" asked Mary Anne. "Shouldn't he or she be in love, too?"

"Well, yes, but not in the same way. His love should be available impersonally to all comers."

"Like a hooker," suggested Mandy.

"Exactly," said Glad. "We must present the same bill of fare year after bloody year and act just as stimulated by it every time. Just like whores."

"Wow, keen," said Howard. "That really gives me renewed reverence for the dignity of my calling."

"But it is sacred," said Glad. "Like the holy prostitutes of ancient Corinth. It's a divine and taboo relationship. So we all have to be careful not to exploit it. That's why it's wrong for Jack Witherspoon to screw Whatsername. Not only is she in a vulnerable position, like a patient or a penitent; it also damages the love relationship that all of us have with all of them."

"I couldn't agree with you more," said Miss Reilly.

"Well, what would you do if you were President Knight?" asked Mandy. "Like, would you fire Jack Witherspoon? And Ruy Blah? And" (she whispered) "Father Bob?"

"Oh my," exclaimed Mary Anne Reilly. "No, of course not. Jack's too valuable a teacher. And it's different with Bob. He's single."

"But isn't that what the moral turpitude clause in the tenure contract means?" asked Howard.

"Oh, I don't know," said Mary Anne. "I suppose if I were the president, I'd talk to them privately. Maybe toss out a few threats. Appeal to their finer feelings . . ."

"That's not what old man Knight's done." Mandy sipped her drink, and waited for the smoke to clear.

"What?"

"What's he done?"

"Omigod, not another flap."

"What has he done this time?"

"Well," said Mandy, rather enjoying the undivided attention, "I don't know exactly what happened with Jack. But Knight told me today to expel C.C. Duxbury. And Jack was in his office today for over an hour. Just before lunch. And Mrs. Pepper was typing a letter to the advisory committee this afternoon, and she covered it up with her hands when I walked into her office."

"Then if she covered it how do you know who it was to?" asked Howard.

"I saw the envelope in her outgoing mail tray later in the day. The good stationery."

Glad grinned. "Oh, Lordy, don't we have the *best* tempests of any teapot you know?"

"Thank God, Knight's leaving," said Mary Anne. "Maybe it will all be forgotten when he goes. Only three months more. You know the faculty. They couldn't possibly put together a fitness hearing committee in that short a time. We'll be arguing about procedures for another year."

"That's for sure," said Mandy.

"By the way," Glad asked Mary Anne, "weren't you supposed to see Knight this afternoon, about your sabbatical?"

"Yes." Mary Anne closed her lips firmly.

"Oh," said Glad.

"Well," Howard asked hurriedly, "how's the search coming? What're the chances for getting somebody really nifty? I teach every afternoon, so I haven't been able to get to any of the sherry parties."

Glad and Mary Anne exchanged glances. As members of the search committee, they had sworn solemn oaths of secrecy.

Miss Reilly spoke. "I believe we can say that we feel quite happy about it so far."

"Rumor has it that the man candidate was a disaster," declared Mandy, fishing for details.

"Well," said Mary Anne, "we've heard that he's a crackerjack administrator on his home turf. But I think we all agreed he might be an unfortunate choice for a women's college."

Howard contributed his morsel of gossip. "I heard that he talked only to the male trustees and totally snubbed you guys and Jane Della Rosa." (The formidable Jane Della Rosa, a motherly-looking Turnbull alumna, had just won a Pulitzer Prize for journalism. She was well-known for her acid tongue.)

Glad chuckled. "That's true. So Ms. Della Rosa asked Mr. Williams if he'd ever had a woman boss. He looked blank for a minute, then said, very pleased with himself, 'Yes, of course, my wife!' "

"Beautiful," said Mandy.

"He also," Glad continued with relish, "devised a swell answer when Mary Anne asked him what he thought of feminism. He said he liked the nice, soft, old-fashioned connotations of the word. Apparently he thought she meant *femininity.* "

"Fantastic," said Mandy. "How was today's woman?"

"Mrs. England? Impressive. We can't really divulge too much. She's in the running."

"I'll tell you about her," put in Bob Bellows. "I was at the candidate's sherry this afternoon."

Glad and Mary Anne maintained a discreet silence while Father Bob described today's woman. He thought her beautiful.

"Beautiful?" asked Mandy. "I mean, isn't she, like, about fifty?"

"Oh, Mandy," cried Barbara Disher angrily. "You're so young sometimes."

"You know what F. Scott Fitzgerald once wrote?" Glad inquired. " 'She was a faded but still beautiful woman of twenty-nine.' "

All the others, except Mary Anne Reilly and Father Bob's silent date, berated Mandy for a while.

"I'm sorry," the Dean of Students said, utterly defeated. "Please go on, Father Bob. What did she look like?"

"Tall, great figure, dark hair, hawk nose, bright blue eyes, sexy low voice."

Barbara asked impatiently, "Is that all you can talk about—her appearance? Would you choose a man president that way?"

"Oddly enough," said Mary Anne, with her usual perfect composure, "that traditionally was a criterion. I don't know if you're familiar with very many college presidents, but I can safely say that one thing they always had in common was striking good looks."

"And three good Anglo-Saxon names," said Howard, nodding. "Our current president is quite typical of the old style."

"Okay," said Barbara Disher, "but I'd like to know more about Mrs. England than how she wore her hair."

"Well," said Father Bob, pausing for a sip of his scotch, "she seemed to have authority. She's a very serious person . . ."

"Humorless, would you say?" asked Howard. "We can't have that."

"I'm not sure. Our questions didn't give her much chance to tell jokes. But she was articulate. Obviously a good administrator. She did 'bottom line' a few times, but otherwise she talks very well."

"Can she raise megabucks?" asked Mandy, flipping her shiny red hair over her shoulder. "That's what matters."

Mary Anne interposed. "Obviously we'd like to know that. But there seems to be no way to judge a person's fund-raising ability in advance. Even Winston Wulff—the bank man on the search committee—admitted that."

"How's her scholarship?" asked Howard. "What's her field?"

"History," said Glad. "She's done a bit of publishing; turned her thesis into a book some time ago. But mostly she's been an administrator, up from the lower ranks at Stott."

"I worry a bit," said Mary Anne, "about people who really like administration. It's the sort of activity that ought to be *forced* on one."

"Yeah," seconded Howard, with feeling. "Anybody who wants to be department chairman is usually the worst possible choice for it. By the way, is Mrs. England still staying in the guest house? We could ring her up and ask her to come on over."

"No," said Glad, "she left right after dinner. Had to catch a plane back to Virginia, so Jane Della Rosa drove her to the Providence airport. Tomorrow's woman is already here. Diane Day, from Osborne College. I have to meet her at nine in the morning and introduce her to the administrators. I thought I'd give her a quick peek at the Pearce pool, too, if there's time. It's so posh."

"Pool!" sang out Barbara Disher from across the room. "Let's go swimming!"

"What—now?" Mary Anne exclaimed in disbelief.

"Sure. Howard has a key. It's great at night. Our kids can stay by themselves, now that Terry's almost twelve."

Glad was dubious. "Won't Prexy see us? His house is right next door. And won't the guard catch us and throw us out?"

"Naw," said Howard. "The night guard's always stewed to the gills."

"Wobbling about on his appointed rounds—protecting all my girls from rapists and murderers." (Glad was surprised to hear Mandy Tweedy say "my girls." Sometimes it was hard to remember that Mandy was actually the Dean of Students. Quite an accomplished one, too.)

"And as for His Majesty," said Barbara Disher, "if he sees lights in the pool he'll think the Oceanids are getting in extra practice for tomorrow's performance. It's illegal, but they do it pretty often. Some of them have keys."

"Beautiful," said Mandy. "So my girls can drown, I mean, in the middle of the night. That would be fun to tell the parents about."

They went. The new natatorium was only a block away. Giggling and whispering and stumbling across the dark campus, the professors invaded the building. The dressing room was strewn with Oceanid costumes and props: baseball mitts and masks, waterproof rubber caps, and an abbreviated uniform for the Oceanid umpire, who, of course, argued with a batter and was pushed into the water in one of the comic bits.

When Glad emerged from the dressing room in one of the college's regulation black cotton tank suits, she paused a moment to watch the others. Mary Anne Reilly was already doing laps and cuddly Barbara Disher was treading water and splashing her husband, who knelt at the side of the pool. Howard had switched on the colored underwater lights. The night seemed pitch-black outside the high windows. The water shimmered as flashes of reflected light danced insanely around on the tiled walls. "What a fantastic place for a Roman orgy," said Glad, exalted. Her voice echoed from wall to wall. "To run from the hot showers into a pool full of icy champagne!"

"Keen!" echoed Howard Disher, slipping his plump body into the pool, and treading water beside Barbara.

Bob Bellows, gorgeous in his tight bathing suit, did a shallow racing dive and chugged across the water noisily. Mary Anne continued her smooth, deliberate breaststroke. Mandy did a fancy dive off the board. "This is *beautiful,*" she shouted from the deep end. "Feels like champagne already!"

Glad folded her glasses, put them on a spectators' bench and immediately walked into a pile of Oceanid equipment—catcher's mitt, paper roses, and baseball bat—lying at the edge of the water. "Damn the Oceanids," she muttered. Her stubbed toe continued to throb as she lowered herself cautiously into the shallow end.

"Oh, it's paradise!" she sang. "I'm glad old Mrs. Pearce gave us this instead of the computer. God bless President Knight! All is forgiven."

"Well," said Mary Anne, continuing her smooth glide.

"Well," said Howard, climbing up to the high board.

"Well," said Mandy, floating on her back.

"I stand corrected," Glad apologized. "Moment of madness."

A frown crossed Howard's face. "Just one thing," he said. "We all have to agree that if one of us drowns, we'll dress him, take him out on Main Street and run him over with a car. Otherwise, you know, they might take away my key." He cannonballed into the water, making a giant splash.

Everyone had class the next day, so they didn't stay very long. The big clock on the high tiled wall said midnight.

Chapter Three

March 15: 8:45 p.m.

DIANE DAY was less nervous than she'd been at the screening interview in Boston. Glad Gold, slightly hung over from Howard's party of the night before, arrived at the guest house a little before 9 A.M. She found the candidate still drinking coffee, so she joined her in a cup. Ms. Day was tiny; she had short hair, curly and thick and brown; her vita said she was 38, but she looked about 30. She was wearing a tailored navy blue suit with a burgundy blouse and burgundy pumps. She looked sharp, and Glad told her so.

Ms. Day laughed with pleasure. "Oh thank you! This is my interview suit; it cost a bundle. I'm so glad someone noticed."

"Would you like to hear about your exciting schedule for today?"

"Sure."

"First, I'll show you the posh Pearce pool. Then I'll take you to Dean Longfellow. His secretary will pass you on to the other administrators. Then Muffy Work, one of our students, a little earnest but a big campus pol, will give you a tour of the campus. After that, lunch with a group of students. Then you face a miscellaneous group of faculty for sherry, and finally dinner with us; then we let you go."

"Fine."

"Is there anything or anyone else you'd like to see, Ms. Day?"

"Sounds exhausting enough already. And please call me Diane. May I call you Gladys?"

Glad smiled ruefully. "Alas, my name is Gladiola. My innocent Midwestern mother thought it was a pretty flower name. Diminutive of Latin *gladius.*"

"Oh yes." Diane Day smiled. "Little sword."

"Feminine gender little sword. But I turned into rather a big one. Anyway, one calls me Glad."

"Now I'll tell you a secret which you mustn't breathe. Diane is my middle name; my real name is *Doris.*"

"Oh wonderful! I can just see the headlines: DORIS DAY NAMED PRESIDENT OF TURNBULL COLLEGE. I bet we'd make the cover of *Time.*"

"Might be worth letting it out for that," mused the candidate. "Well, I suppose we'd better be going."

They rinsed the coffee cups, put on coats, and left the guest house. A cold, windy March morning greeted them, but it was only a short walk past the president's house to the natatorium. Glad had already picked up the key from the main switchboard in Shaw Hall, and she let them in the spectators' entrance. The outer lobby was bright with colorful modern furniture and posters of past Oceanid shows. The smell of chlorine filled the air, and the warm dampness from the pool instantly fogged Glad's cold eyeglasses. "Go on in," she said, blindly pulling out a shirttail to wipe her specs. "I'll be right with you. Can't see a damn thing."

Diane Day's voice echoed loudly, frantically from the next room. "My God, come quickly! Oh my God, there's someone at the bottom of the pool!"

Glad popped on her half-wiped glasses as she ran. She slowed down as she stepped onto the slippery tiles at the pool's shallow end. Next to the edge lay a catcher's mitt, a bunch of paper roses, and a cracked, bloody baseball bat.

"Who *is* that?" asked Ms. Day in a horrified whisper.

"That's the president," said Glad. "Somebody finally did it."

Henderson Neville Knight was fully clothed, in his Harris tweed suit. He was lying facedown, undulating, below the surface of the water but not at the very bottom; his arms were bent, his fingers as swollen as sausages. His handsome silver hair streamed and swirled out darkly in the water. The back of his head was black with clotted blood. The underwater lights were on, and the water sparkled prettily around the dark bundle. The excellent new filtering system kept the water in constant motion, gently animating the lifeless body.

Glad shivered.

"He's facedown," Diane Day observed. "How did you recognize him?"

"He's the only person on campus who wears a suit. Well, almost the only one. I better call the fuzz."

The fuzz came quickly. Murder is not a common occurrence in Wading River, Massachusetts. The most dramatic arrests, listed in the previous year's town report, had been for "marijuana, possession of" (eight arrests); "keeping pigs without a permit" (two); and "lewd and lascivious cohabitation" (one). That last figure had puzzled some townspeople, but there it was.

Acting Chief Alden Chase was only thirty, and insecure. The Wading River force had been lacking a permanent chief for six months. Old Chief Jerry Norton had been awarded early retirement, rather suddenly, for excessive alcoholism (moderate alcoholism would have been tolerated), and the selectmen had been quarrelling among themselves ever since. Selectman Collins wanted his brother, a police sergeant from Attleham, to be appointed chief; selectman Rizzio wanted to hire someone with a big name, preferably Telly Savalas, and selectman Dupont wanted to promote Detective St. Pierre, who was admittedly not one of the brighter men on the force, but had been a semi-pro hockey great, or semi-great, some years earlier. So they had compromised, with undisguised public disappointment, on young, blond Alden Chase, a local boy who had been to college and looked, they said, as if he'd dry up and blow away in a stiff breeze. But he was only an acting chief, he was to understand, until they "worked out their differences."

He stood and looked at the dark undulating form in the water. He was rather in awe of Turnbull people. "Why," he asked the tall, thin, straight-haired woman, "would anyone do a thing like this to a man like him?"

In spite of her shock, Glad couldn't suppress her sad little laugh. "He's the president of a college," she said simply. "Killing the president is the universal academic fantasy. You'd be hard pressed to find any other job in this country which creates more suitable motives for murder."

Chase was startled. "We'd better talk some more, somewhere else," he said. "Soon as the coroner gets here."

"Do you want to talk to me, too?" asked the shorter woman. The cute one in the skirt.

"Sure do. You found the body, right? What's your name? And what's your position here?"

Ms. Day jerked a finger at the corpse. "I'm after his job."

These college people were too much.

The tall woman spoke. "Do you figure somebody bashed him with the bat?"

Chase nodded. "We'll try to get prints, of course. I'm not too hopeful. Unless the guy who did it was unbelievably dumb. Or cuckoo. Hey, you gonna be all right, lady?"

Glad was trembling, though trying to control it. "I

think I had better sit down," she said slowly. "My knees feel weird." There were tears in her eyes. "He wasn't my favorite person, but still . . ."

"It's horrible, isn't it?" Diane Day reached up to put a hand on Glad's shoulder. "Delayed reaction. Officer, do we have to stay here? I mean, can you talk to us later, somewhere more comfortable?"

Alden Chase's boyish face wore a look of concern; he nodded vigorously. "Do you have an office?" he asked the tall, professorish one.

"Sure. Dahl Hall, 124."

"Okay, I can find it. About an hour?"

"Thank you, uh, Chief." (It sounded like something out of a Western movie.)

"Acting chief," he said curtly.

"Oh," said Glad. "Thanks, Acting Chief."

The two women left in a flash.

President Knight was photographed, in and out of water. The wound was on the back of his head, and looked severe enough to have killed him, even if he hadn't been in the pool for God knows how many hours.

The coroner didn't know how many hours. "Quite a few," he said. "He's certainly bloated. We'll have to perform an autopsy. Damn nuisance. You know, Alden, I haven't had an awful lot of experience with murders."

"Join the crowd," said Chase.

A large fat man hurried in through the swimmers' entrance, accompanied by a good-looking blonde in a tennis costume.

"Good, Joe, I was hoping you'd show up," said Chase, nodding to the college chief of security.

The blonde spoke up in a loud, firm voice. "I'm Charlene Christiansen, chairman of physical education. Although of course I don't teach swimming." She stared with frank curiosity at Henderson Knight's no longer handsome body. "I was so relieved to hear it wasn't a student. I mean, we worry a lot about drowning, of course." Her eye caught the split baseball bat, brown with blood among the paper flowers. "Goddamnit," she spurted, "that's one of our good bats."

Alden's face registered his shock. "May I ask what your feelings were toward the deceased?"

"There was no love lost between us. He was trying to get rid of my department. And I never liked him anyway. He struck me as a weak sister."

At least this lady, Alden Chase mused, could never be called a weak sister. She was eying his slight build. Was that gleam in her eye amusement or contempt? Or was he paranoid because of the selectmen's remark—recorded in the minutes and reprinted in the Attleham *Courier-Standard-Star* —about the likelihood of his drying up and blowing away?

"Miss Christiansen—"

"Mrs."

"Pardon me. Mrs. Christiansen, can you tell me how many people have keys to the pool?"

"No one has a key."

"Oh come on, Mrs. Christiansen. Don't answer too fast. Someone must have a key."

"Oh well," she mumbled irritably, "of course, the security guards have one. I figured you knew that. And of course Miss Hallett, the swimming instructor. And there's always one at the main switchboard in Shaw Hall. Oh, and I have one."

"That's all? Did the President have one?"

A momentary look of insecurity crossed her face. "No," she said, less firmly than before. "I don't think so. Maybe he did. Nobody ever tells me anything."

"You see, it's important for us to know. If the president didn't have a key, how'd he get in here?" He turned to Joe Silva.

"I have another one," said Joe. "In addition to the guard's key. The president didn't have one. But they're crazy around here, you know. They just like to think of ways to make my job harder. There could be duplicate keys all over the place. *Professors!* Liberals, you know. Always think the best of everybody. Never lock their offices. Drives you nuts."

The two lawmen shook their heads in mutual sympathy.

"Now," said Chase, "about the guard. Why didn't the night watchman find the body?"

Joe Silva looked uncomfortable. "Well, Alden, it's like this. Goddamned embarrassing, really. The night guard for this part of the campus is this nice old guy, Nick Fowler. Well, fact is, he can't stay off the sauce. Harmless, really. Sixty-four years old. Nice fellah. I guess lately Nick hasn't been too careful about looking where he's supposed to look. Fact is, I fired him yesterday. President's orders. Told him to stop work next Friday. Maybe, what with being canned yesterday, Nick might have got himself a little extra juiced up. You know."

Chase nodded in sympathy. "I want to see him."

"Easy," said Joe. "He lives in Attleham; probably at home right now, sleeping it off."

"Give his address to Patrolman Shirley over there. Al . . ." He spoke to the cop who was dusting the bat for prints. "Hop on over to Attleham and ask Mr. Nick Fowler to come down to the station after lunch. But go easy; he'll be hung over. Don't scare him, and don't tell him what's happened."

The big blonde was standing first on one foot and then the other. "Listen," she said, "do I have to hang around here any longer? I've got a team practice in five minutes."

Chase suppressed irritation. "Would you please write your name, address and phone number in this notebook—just for the record? I may want to talk to you again."

She sighed, and did him the favor.

"You know where to reach me, right?" said Joe Silva.

"Yeah, okay. You can both go; I gotta see a lot of other people."

Silva and Christiansen left together. Her voice could be heard distinctly from the outer lobby. "Looks like you could knock him over with a feather."

Chapter Four

March 15: 10:30 a.m.

ALDEN CHASE found Dahl Hall easily enough. Professor Gold was alone in her small office, reading.

"Ms. Day has gone to Shaw Hall for her interviews," she said. "You know—well, I suppose you don't know—she came down from New Hampshire just for the day, and we decided she'd better try to get in as much of the planned schedule as possible. Of course, she said she'd see you anytime you want. I know where to reach her."

"Maybe I don't need to talk to her after all. You know anything about her?"

Glad smiled. In her briefcase was a fat file on Diane Day and the other finalists. "Pretty much," she said. "She has a doctorate in French, is a full professor and associate dean at Osborne College, is thirty-eight years old, divorced, no children, went to Wheaton—the one in Massachusetts—and Columbia. Just how much do you want to know?"

"Did she know President Knight?"

"No. She'd never seen him before." Glad lit a cigarette.

"Any reason you can think of that she might have wanted him dead? I guess he was definitely leaving Turnbull, wasn't he? No chance of him changing his mind and sticking around?"

"Not a chance. He was going to be vice-president of

the Helmreich Foundation, starting in July. He wanted to go. In fact, it's sort of weird. . . . Well, never mind."

Her dark eyes narrowed briefly behind her big round glasses, and a thoughtful frown momentarily creased her brow. She certainly isn't pretty, he thought. But interesting-looking. Things go on in her head.

"What?" he asked. "What's weird?"

Glad inhaled, and blew out a thoughtful puff of smoke. "Well, one would have thought last year a better time for doing in Prexy. I mean, before he resigned, we were all ready to murder him hourly. Excuse the hyperbole. I mean we were miffed at him a lot. But who'd want to get rid of him now, when he was just about to leave anyway?"

"I was hoping you might help me on that. Tell me about Turnbull personnel who might be involved. Will you?"

Alden Chase had a beautiful smile. Anyway, girls told him so pretty often. So he flashed it on Professor Gold—"attempting to gain the interrogee's confidence," as suggested in Police Law 342 at Jennings County Community College.

Professor Gold smiled back. She had a deep dimple, which made her rather plain face much better looking. "Okay, I'll try, Chief Chase."

"I'm surprised you know my name."

She smiled again. "I read the Attleham *Courier-Standard-Star,* like all good citizens of Wading River. I even went to the famous phone-in-the-john town meeting."

That was embarrassing. In December, there had been a long debate on whether or not the town should appropriate "a sum of money for the purpose of installing a telephone extension in the police station restroom, or take any other action pertaining thereto." Acting Chief Chase had pointed out that often there was only one man on duty at the station house, and that "when you gotta go, you gotta go." The townspeople had loved it. They lavished more debate time on the great phone-in-the-john issue than on the new zoning law. The cops had finally been voted their extension. It had been useful, too, especially during the 24-hour stomach virus in January.

But now Chase was embarrassed, especially when he saw the amusement on the tall woman's rather severe and professorial face. "Did *you* want to murder the president?" he asked bluntly.

She stubbed out her cigarette. "There were times," she admitted. "He was a very rigid person. Old-fashioned. Honorable, no question about that. But ruthless, too, if he thought he was right. Entirely without mercy. Not entirely human. I'm talking too abstractly, aren't I?"

Chase nodded.

"You want a few f'rinstances?"

"That would be helpful. Recent f'rinstances, if possible."

"Well, f'rinstance: one of our faculty members has been rather publicly . . . mm . . . dating a student. Prexy found out, and his instant reaction was apparently to fire 'em both."

Chase opened his little notebook. "What are their names, please?"

Glad looked away from him, stared at the floor. She lit another cigarette; the small office was already almost unbearably smoky. "Please," she said. "I spoke too soon; that was just a rumor. It's confidential. I imagine there's nothing to it."

"Professor Gold," he said gently, "I'm trying to do my job. Murder is serious." A lock of his thin pale hair was falling on his forehead. His shoulders looked frail, but his face was nice, and his voice was confident and pleasant to hear. It was not a low voice, but he spoke distinctly, without slurring, and with only a faint trace of the local accent—the Brockton variant of Bostonese. (When Glad first moved to Wading River, an electrician had mystified her by saying he had located her trouble: she had a shot. A what? A shot. Ess-aitch-oh-ah-tee. Shot Circuit. Glad, being from Cincinnati, was charmed.) Anyway, she was rather a voice nut, and found entirely acceptable the sounds emanating from Chief Chase.

"I'm sorry," she said. "Of course, you have a higher claim. It's common knowledge, anyway: Jack Witherspoon, chairman of the art department, is the man, and the student is Cecilia Duxbury. She's a junior, lives in Boroviak Hall. But Jack is certainly not a murderer. He's the gentlest man possible. One of our most proficient teachers. An innocent man, really; I'm sure she seduced him. It sometimes happens that way."

"Does he have a wife?"

"Yes, sure. Rachel. She's rather a bitch, and often drinks too much, but you have to forgive her. Faculty wives around here are the lowest of the low. With 1100 nubile girls for sex objects, and 50 women Ph.D.s for intellectual companions, the faculty men pay little attention to the wives. They feel snubbed by the liberated women professors and pitied by the students, yet rejected by the town. They haven't much money; they can't find jobs in this small town; they have no status. I don't blame them for being bitchy, or drinking, or whatever. Only a few of them do that; most are surprisingly good-natured. You know, many of these women would be fairly hot stuff on their own: Rachel Witherspoon, for example. She has an MFA from Yale; she's an extremely talented violinist. And Barbara Disher is really an excellent politician."

"Do you think Rachel Witherspoon would kill the president for firing her husband?"

"Of course not. Sooner than Jack would, though."

"Couldn't he find another job? If he's chairman of his department and such a great teacher—"

"That is exactly the problem," said Glad sadly. "Jack gave up scholarship the day he got tenure. He's published nothing since. He's just gotten better at talking and thinking every year. A beloved teacher. And he loves Turnbull; the low-pressure small-towniness of it is just right for him. He hasn't a prayer of finding another job; his like would be destroyed if he had to leave here."

"Well, okay," said Chase, hurriedly scrawling *see Witherspoon* in his little book. "What about the student?"

"C.C.? Oh, she's *nice.* Not too swift in the reading-and-writing department, and maybe a little silly, but really good-natured and pretty and eager. She was the umpire last night—did you see the Oceanid show?"

"No." He had noticed a poster in the supermarket, but town does not attend gown affairs.

"That's a pity. It's free, you know, open to the public. Good thing to take your kids to."

Chase's ex-wife had taken his daughters back to Kansas, but he didn't feel it necessary to tell her this.

"Anyway," Glad continued, "C.C.'s a darling girl. Wouldn't hurt anyone. Loaded with money, I believe."

"Even if the president had expelled her?"

"Oh, expulsion doesn't mean so much here. The girl who flunks out, or the occasional one who's canned for social reasons usually goes to Europe for a year; then we let her back in."

"But if her parents would be angry with her about this—and if she's silly as you say, and if she tried to beg the president to reconsider and he refused—"

Glad took a long time crushing out her cigarette. "Well," she said, "she does spend a good deal of time in the pool. And she certainly knows how to handle a baseball bat. No, I can't believe it. Simply impossible. She's in my Victorian poets class; she says that

Tennyson 'turns her on.' She couldn't have bashed Prexy."

Chase didn't see why admiration for Tennyson proved one incapable of murder, but apparently Miss Gold was convinced. Crazy. She was lighting *another* cigarette.

"You smoke too much," he said.

She inhaled deeply, turned her face ostentatiously away from him, and exhaled a great cloud. "You get much use out of that phone in your john?" she asked.

"Okay, okay," he said. "Back to the money angle. Do you know if President Knight was unusually well fixed?"

"I believe he was well off. Of course, that gorgeous house comes with the job. But if you're thinking about Mrs. Knight, you can forget it; poor woman, she's an absolute saint. Perfect president's wife. Has a tendency to finish your sentences for you, but otherwise a dear. Besides, why would she take Prexy to the pool to do him in, when she could just slip something in his coffee at home?"

"To make it look as though somebody else did it, of course."

"Ah," said Glad enthusiastically. "I see you read murder mysteries too."

"You know," he said, "you really do smoke an awful lot."

"One thing puzzles me," she said innocently. "Will you be conducting this investigation personally? Or do you think the selectmen will want somebody from outside—you know, Jack Webb or somebody?"

"I guess they will," he said, "when they hear the details. But an outsider would cost money; there'd have to be a special town meeting to approve it. So for now, Wading River and Turnbull College will have to make do with me. . . . By the way, I'm sorry if I nagged you about smoking."

"I'm sorry if it bothers you," she said humbly. "I'll open the window."

"Now, so far you've given me a list of five people who couldn't possibly have killed your proxy."

"Prexy."

"Prexy. Do you want to tell me about any others who couldn't have done it?"

"You see," she said, "it's hard to imagine any of us doing it. To imagine it's even been done." But as she spoke, the picture formed again—the proper dark tweed suit lying, half dangling almost at the pool bottom, the bloated fingers, ever-so-slightly moving in the sparkling, constantly circulating water, the once-glorious mop of snowy hair streaming around the broken head, brown with clotted blood.

Glad twitched involuntarily.

"I know," said Chase. "It wasn't right."

"No."

"You said that lots of people had motives for killing him."

"Okay," she sighed, and did not light another cigarette. "None of these will sound serious enough for murder, but this is a small, passionate world. The two people in Italian, a department he abolished last year. But they've left Wading River. Howard Disher, untenured, poli sci, fired by Prexy. Can't find another job. This is his last semester. And, I suppose, his wife Barbara. Bob Bellows, the chaplain, if the old man had known about *his* affairs with students . . . ! Then there's Charlene Christiansen and all her department—I think there are six instructors; Knight was getting ready to dump gym. Mary Anne Reilly—I guess she's another possibility, particularly if she really was denied a sabbatical. Poor thing, after thirty-some years of selfless devotion to Turnbull, when she'd finally really got on to something about double-stars . . ."

"Totally incapable of murder, of course?"

"Of course. How dare you! Let me go on: George

Cramer, biology, whom Knight fired last year for smoking grass at a student party. But he's gone, found another job. The Dean, Bruce Longfellow, who is rumored to fight with Prexy all the time. Mandy Tweedy, the Dean of Students, who was publicly reprimanded by you-know-who for wearing jeans to a faculty meeting. Irma Freundlich, poli sci, who may have decided Prexy's in on a Communist takeover. Mrs. Pepper, the president's executive secretary, and who is in love with him . . ."

Chase stopped writing. "God, maybe the selectmen had better hire James Bond. Tell me one thing, though."

"Sure."

"Do you know anybody who had a key to the pool, outside of the guards, Joe Silva, the switchboard, and the gym people?"

"Well, I've heard that some students have them. I don't know that for sure. And . . ."

"Yes?"

"Howard Disher. But please let me say this . . ."

"A saint?"

Her dimple showed again. "How did you guess? The archetypal Boy Scout. Mr. Goodkid. I mean, have you *seen* him? He's a teddy bear. The sort of grown-up boy who says 'keen!' and 'nifty!' Absolutely incapable."

"Thanks. He's the one who was fired?"

"Last year, to pacify Irma Freundlich, his chairperson, who's a nut. He's still here, but hasn't found a job yet. Umm, speaking of Howard, I guess you'll want to know that a group of us were swimming last night. We used his key."

"You did *what?*"

"Yeah. After a party. We were drunk."

"What time was this?"

"Oh, I guess from about 11:30 till midnight. Maybe 12:15. All very innocent, no skinny-dipping. No sign of Prexy, either."

"Is it possible that Mr. Disher forgot to lock the door when you left?"

Glad thought a second. "I'm not absolutely sure. I think I remember seeing him lock up, but I'm probably a fairly unreliable eyewitness."

"Well, thank you very much." He gave her a helping of his surefire smile. "I'd better go see some other people. I may want to talk to you again. And would you please call if you think of anything else I should know?"

"Sure," she said cheerfully. "But when you answer the phone, I don't want to know what room you're in."

He stood up, ready to leave. She got up too. She was a good three inches taller than he. At least, he thought, she didn't say anything about blowing away in a stiff breeze.

Glad was surprised at how likable the young chief had been. Like many academics, she pigeonholed policemen with slaughterhouse workers, career soldiers, and that unfortunate town official whose duty it is to put stray dogs to sleep. All necessary jobs—God knows, *she* couldn't do those things—but one couldn't help pondering what sort of person would choose such professions. Well. Alden Chase seemed okay. Attractively wispy. Leslie Howardish. Maybe even smart.

It was 11:07. She had a freshman writing class at 11:30; fortunately it was already prepared. She would hand back last week's papers, give the girls a stern little talk about participles and other easily mislaid modifiers, then would cheer them up with some praise: most of the girls were writing much more clearly. She was gratified.

After lunch Muffy Work would be bringing Diane Day to the faculty lounge, where poor Diane would be facing the faculty at its worst. Altogether too many had been showing up for these "informal" sherries, and asking such pointed questions that the search committee was beginning to fear all their finalists would drop out of the running. Ferenczi wanted each candidate to be a Nobel Prize–winning scholar. Bob Bellows wanted to extract a promise from each to strengthen the tutorial system. Fatherly old Cabot Coale, a gray eminence in history, wanted to know if each had spiritual values in harmony with the intentions of Turnbull's puritan founders. Irma Freundlich had been trying to sniff out associations with Commie-front organizations. And several of the male professors had been accusing each woman candidate of being weak on fund-raising experience. Of course, that was true: traditionally women had not been allowed to raise funds; all the female finalists were rather on the academic side of deanship. But one always presumed that a smart, businesslike, energetic woman could learn to raise money. Didn't one?

Lucille Walker England gained points on that score. A bit glib, but very smooth. She had handled herself well, particularly on the tough stuff about finances. Ms. Rosen had simply laughed at the committee's ruder questions. They deserved it; but perhaps, in this case, laughter wasn't the ideal response. Was Diane Day strong enough to stand up to the second-round interrogation?

God, thought Glad, we are a bunch of killers sometimes.

Well, what to do before class? Only a few minutes. She could answer the letter from her father, a jeweler in Cincinnati, or—yes, there was just time enough to write a reply to that nice man in Australia, Professor Crumb, who asked for a reprint of the "Tithonus" article in *PMLA*.

Glad got a sheet of letterhead stationery from a desk drawer, and took the dust cover off her typewriter. How strange.

There was a piece of lined, three-hole notebook pa-

per stuck in her typewriter. The handwriting was
not familiar to her. The message was brief:

Dear Proffessor Gold: C.C. Duxbury cheats.
She plegarized her last paper in your class.

It was written with a felt-tip pen, with brown ink.
There was something revolting about it. Like dried
blood on a paper flower.

Chapter Five

March 15: 1:30 p.m.

"DO YOU TAKE cream and sugar?" asked Mrs. Henderson Neville Knight, whose first name was Melanie.

"No, thanks," replied Alden Chase.

"The strudel is really excellent. I hope you'll help yourself," she said, smiling anxiously.

Melanie Knight was plump and pretty, fiftyish, gray-haired, big-bosomed. She was wearing dark slacks and a Chinese-looking silk jacket. Her home—the president's house—was, as Glad had described it, marvelous, even more impressive inside than out, full of thick oriental rugs, gleaming mahogany, red leather, paintings with ornate gold frames. Little silver things were everywhere—candlesticks, dishes, vases—and there were flowers all over the place.

Opulent, thought Chase, who had grown up in the Lakeside section of Wading River, where the poor folk lived in bungalows which had once been summer cottages. Lake Ellen was still beautiful, but now hopelessly polluted by the sewage piped into it by the neighboring town of Foxton. The people who lived in Lakeside were either the most recently arrived Portuguese, usually destined to prosper and move to better parts of Wading River—or the old, settled, hardcore Yankee poor, who were often destined to live there on welfare till the bloody end. The rows

of closely packed mailboxes bore a fine collection of
sturdy old English and Scottish names; the tiny un-
heated houses bore an equally impressive collection
of unemployed alcoholics and other failures, de-
serted mothers with too many children, young ad-
dicts, pregnant teenagers, incompetent burglars,
and the wretched old. Alden Chase had lived all his
life in this white Anglo-Saxon Protestant neighbor-
hood, and he found the Knight home almost over-
whelming. Wonder if all this goes with the job. Isn't
another house like this in Wading River—surprising
they've never been hit. Probably have a good alarm
system.

Mrs. Knight was nervous, yet eager to please. So
eager, in fact, that she tended to nod and say
"mm-hm" all the time Chase was talking.

"By the way," she interrupted, "what did my husband die from? The drowning or the blow on the
head?"

"We won't know that till we get the report on
the . . ."

". . . autopsy," she said, nodding earnestly. "Yes,
of course, mm-hm, I see."

"Now, Mrs. Knight, I'm afraid it's my duty to ask
you a few . . ."

". . . few questions? Certainly. Go ahead." Her
sweet round face assumed a look of polite expecta-
tion.

"I know this is a painful . . ."

". . . painful time for me? Yes, of course it is, but
you should do your duty."

Chase felt uncomfortable. He really couldn't abide
having his sentences finished for him, but she was *so*
eager to please, so smilingly anxious. It would be
wrong to be rude to a nervous widow, wouldn't it?
Unforgivable.

"Did you and President Knight have a happy . . ."

". . . marriage?" she asked.

". . . marr, uh, life together?" he concluded firmly.

She nodded understandingly. "I see why you have to ask that. The answer is yes. We had a very comfortable arrangement. I wouldn't call it really romantic, but we needed each other. I was—well—helpful to him, socially. I love giving parties; I'm good at it. I get along with people. I suffer fools happily, willingly, all the time. I like faculty members, and students, and secretaries, and gardeners—and I have loved this house. And particularly the greenhouse—did you notice the carnations? And the rose garden?"

Her plump face was full of pride as she glanced around the elegant living room; her anxiety had lessened visibly.

"Were you looking forward to . . ."

". . . to moving? To New York? Would *you?* After this?"

"But wouldn't you have been able to live well in New York, too?"

"Too? Oh, we'd still have been well off, of course. But I, I loved it here. They kill people in New York, you know."

"They kill people in Wading River, too." He regretted this tactless remark as soon as he made it, but Melanie Knight went right on as if he had not spoken.

"The sidewalks are covered with doggie-doo. I don't know anyone in New York. Not a soul. All of my friends are in New England. My work—here—entertaining, keeping this place nice, supervising the greenhouse, all this . . ."

She couldn't continue. Tears welled in her eyes. For the greenhouse—not for her husband.

"I'm sorry, Mrs. Knight. But now you won't have to go to New York after all, will you?"

She managed a nervous laugh. "I see what you mean. I could have drowned Henderson to keep from going to New York? I see. Yes. That's plausible."

Her coffee cup rattled in its saucer as she picked it up.

"I don't think," said Chase gently, "that anyone would regard that as a very likely . . ."

". . . motive? I'm glad to hear that. But I must admit that I have been angry with Henderson for resigning, for taking that foundation job. It's no secret; there has been a coolness between us. For some time."

"Did anyone else know about this . . ."

". . . coolness?"

". . . *difficulty* between you and your husband?"

She spoke firmly: "Mrs. Pepper, his secretary, I'm sure. She knew everything about Henderson. She wanted to go to New York; that's the funny thing. She was upset because he didn't ask her." She picked a minuscule crumb from her full bosom, and dropped it into a gleaming crystal ashtray.

Aha, thought Chase. He wanted to flash his famous smile on her, but decided it would be inappropriate.

"Is Mrs. Pepper currently unmarried, then?"

"Widowed for years. The office wife, you know."

"Did she—do you think—this is awkward, but do you think they might have been . . ." He paused, waiting for her to fill in the blank.

"Might have been what?"

Can't win, he thought. Habitual blank-fillers never do it when you want them to. "Might have been lovers?"

"Pretty Polly Pepper?" She smiled ironically. "I doubt it. But she certainly adored him. Thought he was the Almighty."

"Do you think it's possible that she might have . . ."

". . . killed him? From jealousy? Because he wouldn't take her to New York? I see what you mean. Yes. I think that's entirely possible."

Melanie Knight looked distinctly pleased. She helped herself to a second strudel.

After a pause, Chase spoke suddenly. "Mrs. Knight, did you or your husband get much use out of the . . ."

". . . pool?"

Chase smiled. "Now, how did you guess that I was going to say pool?"

She motioned to him that her mouth was too full of strudel to speak. Chase waited patiently.

She swallowed, and spoke slowly. "I guess it's natural that you should be interested in details about the pool. Considering. You know, officer, I am not unintelligent. Even though my activities are entirely domestic, and I've never been paid for my work."

"I didn't mean—I didn't mean to imply . . ."

"I'm sure you didn't." She smiled sweetly. "Why don't you have another strudel? You look as though you might . . ."

". . . might dry up and blow away?" he interposed triumphantly.

". . . could use the extra calories, which *I* can't." She smiled. "Anyway, I have been inside the pool building, but I don't swim. Henderson was a fine swimmer, and often used the pool when it wasn't occupied. But he didn't have a key. There's one at the switchboard, which is open twenty-four hours a day."

"And Mrs. Pepper? Does she use the pool?"

"I have no idea what Polly Pepper does in her spare time," she said calmly. "Are you sure you won't have more coffee?"

"Quite sure, thanks." He rose. "I really must be going. You've been very . . ."

". . . helpful." She nodded. "I'm glad to have met you, Officer Chase. And I want you to know that I have faith in you. I'm sure you'll soon find out who committed this terrible crime. May I show you the rose garden on your way out?"

"That would be ni . . ."

". . . nice," she said, nodding vigorously. She led him through a French door into a perfectly clipped formal garden, and pointed out, along the flagstone path, her prize-winning Tropicanas, her most productive Paul Grays, her wonderfully deep-toned Oklahomas, her rather disappointing John F. Kennedys (subject to mildew and blackspot), and her breathtaking but delicate Royal Mel Averys. All were leafless, dry bundles of prickly sticks, protruding from little mounds of dirt and garden trash, still deep in their winter coma. The path led to an iron gate in a decorative fence, and thence to the Pearce Memorial Pool.

Glad Gold, Mary Anne Reilly, and Olympia Principe (professor of music) sat in the faculty lounge after lunch. They were waiting for Muffy Work, a junior, to deliver their latest presidential candidate for the slaughter. The three women constituted the elected faculty members of the search committee; they had grown close during the months of endless résumé-reading, driving to Boston for preliminary interviews, and caucusing about faculty needs and sore points—all in preparation for their meetings with the trustee members of the committee.

Of course, the murder was a major topic, and they had already speculated and deplored and gossiped for a while about that, but they knew that it would be *the* topic in any campus gathering for weeks to come, so finally Olympia suggested that they *try* to talk about something else.

Olympia was a pianist and harmony teacher in her late forties, married to a famous neurosurgeon. In contrast to Mary Anne Reilly's comfortable sixty-ish plumpness and Glad Gold's thin tallness, Olympia Principe's looks were extreme, abetted by clouds of flamboyant, probably touched-up black hair, huge dark eyes and a voluptuous figure.

She was telling her Wanda Landowska story. "When Wanda arrives at Nadia Boulanger's apartment, Nadia isn't quite ready to go out, so she says, 'I'll only be a minute, Wanda dear. Make yourself comfortable: play the piano or the harpsichord or the organ.' "

"I love this joke already," said Glad with enthusiasm.

"So," said Olympia, dragging on her cigarette, "Wanda plays a little Bach on the organ. Suddenly she comes rushing into Nadia's bedroom, carrying a small white rubber object."

"I hope Muffy doesn't arrive before the punch line," said Mary Anne.

Olympia smiled, and put on a vaguely Slavic accent: " 'Nadja, my darlink,' says Wanda, 'Vot is dis leetle white ting?' 'Oh,' says Nadia, 'I found that in the Bois de Boulogne one day. It came in a little American-made package, and it said on it "Place on your organ to prevent disease." So I put it on the organ, and I haven't had a cold since.' "

Professors Gold and Reilly laughed enthusiastically.

"Now," said Olympia, "what else can we talk about?"

"The murder," said Glad.

"*No,*" said Olympia, "I refuse to dwell on this nasty business. At this rate, we'll all start to feel that he was a good old president, after all, and that would be silly and wrong."

"I agree," said Mary Anne. "*Nil nisi bonum,* but we must remember we don't want another Henderson Neville Knight. What do you suppose is keeping our candidate?"

"Maybe Muffy's showing her the dorms," suggested Glad.

"By the way, what do you think of Muffy?" asked Mary Anne.

"She's certainly worked hard in this committee," answered Glad, without much enthusiasm.

"I don't like her," said Olympia with finality.

"Why's that?"

"I had her for intermediate piano. She's a disgusting . . . what do they call it? Brown-noser. Every time she hasn't been practicing she goes into ecstasy about how wonderfully I play, like an angel, and how truly great a teacher I am."

"She's a politician," said Mary Anne. "But smart. One of our brightest girls, they say. And cute as a button, with that curly blond hair."

"Oh, Mary Anne," said Glad, "you never want to believe anything bad about any of our students."

"Well, what do you have against Muffy?"

"Nothing major. But I must admit her self-righteousness irritates me. The way she always sides with us or the administration against the students. She's such a model Turnbull woman—vice-president of college government, head judge on judicial board, lecturing the freshmen on the sacredness of the honor system and all that. In short, a fink."

"I agree," said Olympia. "She's really impressed our committee trustees, though, with all that flattery. If you ask me, she's a junior league Henderson Knight."

"God, you're right," said Glad.

"Now what shall we talk about?" asked the musician. "Have you heard the one about the greyhound?"

"Yes!" the other two shouted.

"Am I early?" asked Howard Disher, entering the faculty lounge from the coat room. "My students are taking a midterm, so I thought I'd come and hear today's woman."

Mary Anne patted the sofa beside her. "Sit right here, Howard," she said warmly. "You are a bit early, but we expect our little Muffy to bring Ms. Day at any moment."

Howard smiled and plumped his shaggy teddy-bear self down beside the astronomer.

There was a silence.

"Well," said Glad.

"Well," said Howard. "What's the word on the . . . um . . . accident in the pool? Anyone arrested yet?"

The women looked distressed. Olympia said, "We felt exhausted on that particular subject, so we were—I blush to admit it—telling jokes."

"Oh, keen!" said Howard, lighting up. "You know, Barb and I have to collect a lot of jokes in a hurry. You knew that, didn't you?"

"No," said Olympia. "Are we allowed to ask why?"

"Our daughter Terry is going to be twelve next week and all her life, every time she was hurt because we refused to explain something to her or to repeat some crudity we were laughing at, Barb and I would say, 'We'll tell you when you're twelve.' "

"Oho!" cried Glad. "And she remembered?"

"Yes. The day of reckoning is at hand. She informed us last week that she was truly looking forward to her birthday, when we'd entertain her with an almost endless collection of real nifty smut. Of course, we don't *remember* any of the things we promised we'd tell her, so now we're frantically trying to amass an anthology of filth."

"Knock knock," said Glad suddenly.

"Who's there?" asked Howard.

"Fuck," said Glad.

"Fuck who?" asked Howard promptly.

"Fuck who*m*," said Glad primly. "That's an English department joke."

"I'm not sure if it will do," mused Howard. "I'll try it on Barb tonight."

"I've got a riddle," said Olympia. "Why is the Amtrak Metroliner like a childless husband?"

"I give up," said Howard.

"Because it always pulls out on time."

"No," said Mary Anne firmly.

"Olympia!" said Glad. "The fact that it's a riddle doesn't make it suitable for Howie's innocent little girl."

"Oh well," said Olympia, slightly hurt, "I think American children are overprotected in these matters. Parents and teachers giving them solemn lectures about sexuality and all that. Much healthier to learn it in the gutter, I say. Are you going to tell the kid the greyhound joke?"

At that moment, Muffy Work appeared, leading Diane Day and talking with bubbly enthusiasm about what an exemplary faculty Turnbull College possessed.

"And these," concluded Muffy, pointing to Olympia, Glad and Mary Anne, "are my three favorite professors. Dr. Principe is just the greatest pianist ever, and Dr. Gold is the most enthusiastic, funny English professor, and Dr. Reilly—well, actually, I didn't take astro for my science, but all the kids say she's really heavy duty."

The three women looked embarrassed, but Diane Day saved them with some happy comments about her tour of the campus.

Faculty began to drift in: the atmosphere gradually changed to one of formality, then minimally concealed hostility as the questions began.

"Mrs. Day," said one of the political scientists, "you look extremely young. And you've spent your entire rather brief career, as I understand it, at Osborne. Do you really have the contacts—in business, government, finance, that sort of thing—that the president of a college needs in order to raise money?"

She was splendid on that one; it turned out that, in fact, she did have foundation contacts and had negotiated a sizable grant for faculty development at Osborne.

Ferenczi, as usual, asked about scholarly publica-

tions. Diane Day's were skimpy and a bit bizarre for
an administrator—poems in little reviews—but she
admitted as much, disarmingly.

Several of the women asked feminist questions.
Ms. Day had impeccable credentials in that area.

Silver-haired Cabot Coale, puffing on his pipe,
asked how she stood on spiritual values.

For the first time, Diane Day looked nonplussed.
"Spiritual values? I'm for them, of course."

Cabot launched into a few silver-tongued remarks
on the decline of morality since his student days.
"Miss Day, if you were to become president of Turnbull, would you plan to install a lover in the president's house?"

Several faculty members protested; Cabot insisted
the question was highly relevant, considering the
permissive climate these days, and the obvious at-
tractiveness of the candidate.

Glad found herself shaking with embarrassed
rage. She thought: he can't bear the idea that a
woman—not an aged nun but a real woman—might
be his boss.

Diane Day just laughed good-naturedly. "I was
prepared for this," she said. "I have a good friend—
also female and divorced—who has been a candidate
for several college presidencies. She warned me that
there's always someone on every faculty who wants
to know if you'll have a lover in the president's
house."

"Well," persisted Cabot, "will you"—puff, puff—
"have one?"

She smiled calmly. "I don't underestimate the
need for discretion and a dignified image in a college
president, and I don't think your concern is irrele-
vant. I understand it. But I would say that whatever
happens behind the president's closed doors, her
choice of friends, for example, is no one's business
but the president's. I'm sure you would want the pri-
vacy of your home to be similarly inviolate."

Someone applauded. Cabot Coale looked sour and went on puffing.

Good lady, thought Glad. Mary Anne Reilly whispered to Olympia, "As different as Knight and Day."

Chapter Six

March 15: 3:00 p.m.

WHEN ALDEN CHASE got back to the station, he found four messages waiting for him.

The first was that Dr. Plantar had finished the autopsy and would like the chief to call him. The second was that Nick Fowler, the supposedly hung-over ex-security guard, was not in his apartment; there was no sign that he had slept in his bed, and his landlady told Patrolman Albert Shirley that she thought it was funny she hadn't seen old Nick since he had left for work the day before. The third message indicated that there had been another outbreak of mailbox overturnings last night. The fourth was that a Professor John Witherspoon was waiting in the chief's office.

Chase asked Al Shirley to look for Fowler. "Get a description from Joe Silva, then make the rounds of the bars," he advised. "Also, give the boys in Attleham and Foxton a call, ask them to look for a sixtyish guy, maybe drunk, maybe wearing a security guard's uniform. The Turnbull guards don't carry guns; I doubt he's dangerous. Even if he did use a baseball bat on Henderson Knight. But if he doesn't turn up by—say—four o'clock, we'd better send out an all-state description."

"Right, Chief. Anything else?"

"About three thirty, when school's out, go see

Jimmy and Scotty Letts, over on Clinger Street, and ask them if they know it's a federal crime to deface a mailbox."

"Okay, Chief."

Since he didn't want to see Professor Witherspoon yet, Chase used a phone at the main reception desk to call Doc Plantar, the coroner's physician.

Peter Plantar, the only doctor in Wading River, was actually a dermatologist. Since he was seldom called on to perform as coroner's physician, he brought considerable enthusiasm to the job, which he found a refreshing change from adolescent acne and detergent-caused eczema. It was, in fact, a little hard to turn him off. His last post had been on a car accident victim, and had included a lengthy description of the victim's incipient gallstones, severe dental caries and badly sewn old appendectomy scar.

"I'm really glad you called, Chief Chase," said the doctor. "This was a fascinating post, really wonderful."

"That's great," said Alden, gnawing on a number 2 pencil. "Can you summarize your report for me?"

"Sure enough," said Plantar. "At ten thirty A.M. on March fifteen, at Leggett's Funeral Home, I, Peter Plantar, M.D., coroner's physician of Wading River, Massachusetts, examined the body of Henderson Neville Knight, President of Turnbull College. The body appeared to be that of a well-nourished, muscular man, about fifty years of age; it was five-feet-nine and one-half inches long, and the estimated weight . . ."

"Doc . . ."

"Yes, Chief?"

"Can you summarize? You know, like skip the ingrown toenails and the normal healthy liver and the dandruff, and tell me what killed him?"

"Well, that's really the fascinating part," said the doctor, undaunted. "You know, I'm not really absolutely sure whether it was the blow on the head or the drowning. May I read you something, please?"

"If you must." Chase chewed away on his pencil.

"It's really interesting."

"Go ahead."

"I'm quoting from Dr. Norman Beck Kricher's *Autopsy: Diagnosis and Modern Technique*. He says, here on page forty-five, 'It is perhaps not easy to determine whether a body which is found in water was drowned or may have died of some other cause when it was submerged after death. . . .' You see, in cases like this, some lungs will contain water, or at least traces. Just as often the lungs won't show traces of water. Fascinating, huh?"

"Yeah," said Chase, who had gotten a piece of pencil lead in his mouth and didn't like the taste much. "Did Knight have water in his lungs?"

"Yes. And in the stomach. Which points to drowning. But you see, it could have entered after death. And he did have a fractured skull, and intracranial hemorrhaging. On the other hand, there seemed to be petechial hemorrhages on the skin, which would seem to indicate asphyxia—at least according to the monograph I read by Jackiw and Seubert—and yet, he was awfully bloated, you know, from being in the water so long. Now there's another scholar . . ."

"How long?"

"Well, that's another really interesting question. The cold water perhaps had some effect on the development of rigor . . ."

"You mean you can't say?"

"Well, the corneas were becoming opaque. That probably means six to ten hours. However . . ."

"You'd say, then, he was killed maybe between midnight and four A.M.?"

There was a moment of silence.

"Doc?"

"Well, I hate to commit myself to anything so specific. But—all right. That's a reasonable conjecture."

"And would you say the skull fracture indicates that only a strong person could have wielded the bat?"

"Well, perhaps. Or, more likely, an angry person. Or a very determined one."

Chase sighed very softly. "Oh well. Anything else I should know? Left-handed batter? Arsenic in the liver? Somebody else's blood on the bat?"

"Well, no. But Mr. Knight had been operated on, successfully, for a duodenal ulcer."

"Thanks, Doc."

"You see what I mean about it being a fascinating case? Now Pearson, Pastra-Landis and Epstein wrote a report in which . . ."

"Yeah. I'll call you again, before the inquest."

"Anytime. Delighted. Really."

Chase still didn't relish going in to see Witherspoon so he spent a few minutes at the front desk, looking over the list of yesterday's routine crimes and violations. One speeder, an Attleham resident. Two illegally parked cars on Main Street, one from Wading River in front of a hydrant, one from Rhode Island, parked after midnight. And the serious federal case of the mailbox-overturning on Clinger Street, of course. One failure to signal on making a left turn. One homicide.

Chase went into his office, and found a tall, gray-haired man reading the station copy of Vogler's *Manual of Police Procedure.* The professor put the book down hastily, sprang to his feet, and vigorously shook hands with the police chief.

"I'm delighted to meet you," he said with an enthusiasm that may have been phony but didn't seem so. "I walked over from the college and was surprised at how short a walk it was. Only five minutes or so . . ."

"Yes?"

"Yes. You know, I've never been here before. It's certainly a fascinating place—something macho about it, and primal, yet queerly old-fashioned and cozy, too. Like an old railroad station, or a Western Union office. The smell of stale cigar smoke, maybe . . ."

"Sergeant Ruby smokes cigars. Also, two of the selectmen. They come in a lot."

Witherspoon rambled on; Alden Chase waited patiently, wondering, with some envy but more simple curiosity, how a man like this could possibly be attractive to one of those young, beautiful, rich Turnbull girls. It couldn't just be the height, could it? Otherwise, Witherspoon didn't seem to have much to recommend him. Long, wavy, blondish gray hair; a wispy, darker beard; round wire-rimmed glasses; heavily lined, very thin face; narrow shoulders; faded plaid flannel shirt; no tie; wrinkled corduroy pants; scuffed loafers. A mess. Haggard-looking. And he talked on and on, about nothing.

"Professor Witherspoon . . ."

"Yes?"

"Come to the point."

"Yes, yes, of course." Witherspoon took off his glasses, pulled out a handkerchief, and started polishing. "You see," he said, "I have a lot of trouble talking meaningfully in here. It's so quiet. And light."

"Quiet? And light?" Chase was mildly nonplussed.

"I'm an art history teacher. That's really the only thing I do in life. And I always lecture with slides, of course. In a semi-dark room, with the projector fan whirring. It's gotten so that's the only time I can talk easily . . . I sometimes think there's a hidden connection between the projector and my mouth. When the lights dim and the machine goes on, the mouth opens and words come out. Once the projector broke down and I couldn't finish the class. Had to let 'em go a half hour early. I've really got a screw loose."

Chase chuckled. "I'll pull the shade, if it would

help. And the air conditioner would make a humming sound, like your projector. But I think it's a bit chilly for that, don't you?"

"Seriously, it might make all the difference. A bit of a whir or hum, a little darkness. I'm eccentric. I admit it."

"You're a fruitcake." Chase laughed as he drew the shade and turned on the air conditioner.

"That's better," said Witherspoon, smiling faintly. "I thought you'd want to see me, since I should be your prime suspect for the murder of that son-of-a-bitch. Assuming that you've already heard some of this, I've decided to tell you the whole truth about everything."

"Good thought," said Chase, rolling a new pencil back and forth between his thumb and forefinger.

"To put it as simply as possible, I can't stand my wife, who is smart and lovely to look at, but a bitter, jealous drunk. Cecilia Duxbury, a junior, is beautiful and warm and touchingly innocent. I've made a perfect ass of myself about her. Everyone on campus has seen us holding hands—and yesterday that son-of-a-bitch called me to his office and gave me the opportunity to resign at the end of the school year. I refused. We argued. He said he would institute a fitness hearing. Since I'm tenured, the only way I can be fired is to be found guilty, by a faculty hearing committee, of either incompetence or moral turpitude."

"Moral turpitude, eh?" asked Chase. Witherspoon nodded, smiling faintly.

"We don't get too many arrests for that in Wading River," commented the chief. "But I expect it's the same as our 'lewd and lascivious.' "

"Precisely," said the professor.

"Would this hearing committee convict you?"

"I don't see how they could fail to. I am guilty. And my colleagues are men and women of honor."

"So," said Chase, tapping his pencil on the desk, "you killed Knight."

"No." Witherspoon's lined face was impassive.

"Did you threaten him?"

"I told him I was getting a lawyer."

"What time was this meeting, and did you see Knight again after the meeting?"

Witherspoon stroked his beard. "I went to his office just before lunch. Maybe twelve fifteen After that meeting I never saw the son-of-a-bitch again. May he rot in hell." There was a look of pain on Witherspoon's thin face, but his voice remained calm and musical.

Chase chewed his pencil thoughtfully. "Strong language."

"I've called him that before. The son-of-a-bitch was all principle; had no human feelings at all. Fired a nice young fellow, Howard Disher, just to keep peace with Irma Freundlich, the campus crazy. Fired another good guy last year for smoking pot. Not only denied Mary Anne Reilly her sabbatical, but insulted and humiliated her, only yesterday. Told her she was too old to produce scholarly work of any value to Turnbull. One of the brightest people we have. Son-of-a-bitch."

"Did you feel like killing him?"

"Of course," said Witherspoon, lifting his glasses with his left hand, and rubbing the bridge of his nose with his right. "But I didn't. Hell, I may be guilty of moral turpitude, but I'm basically a decent soul. At the time the son-of-a-bitch was killed, I was home with my lovely wife—watching her throw up, holding her hand while she had hysterics about our future, putting her to bed when she passed out. She may even remember some of it; you should check with her."

Chase spat out a piece of pencil. "Just what time was that? When the son-of—when Knight was killed."

Witherspoon smiled. "I assume," he said evenly, "that it was shortly after the faculty swimming party which I had the misfortune to miss. Must have been twelve-thirty or later."

"Oh, yeah. Well, who do you think *did* kill him?"

"Oh, hell, how do I know? Anybody. Maybe an *ad hoc* committee."

"Do you have a key to the swimming pool?"

Was there a hint of consternation added to Witherspoon's already anxious-looking face? At any rate, it took him several seconds to reply, while the air conditioner buzzed comfortably. "Well, that is something I don't have," he said finally. "Almost nobody has one. Except Howard Disher. And the guards, and the switchboard lady."

"Well, thanks much for coming in, Professor."

"You're welcome. Any time."

Witherspoon left. Mary Donnelly, Wading River's policewoman, came in a few seconds later.

"Sparky just called," she said. "Nick Fowler, that security guard, has been caught. In Foxton. Trying to board a bus for Logan Airport. Al Shirley's bringing him in."

"Maybe I won't have to deal with any more of these fruitcakey, complicated professorial types. Maybe it's all wrapped up."

"Jeez, it's cold in here," Mary exclaimed.

The air conditioner whirred away. It was a soothing sound.

Chapter Seven

March 16: 12:30 p.m.

LEADERLESS Turnbull College continued to run as smoothly as the eponymous Wading River, which ambles placidly through its town, undisturbed by rocks thrown into it by kids on the Main Street Bridge. March 16th, the day after the murder, the dining halls served a choice of tuna-noodle casserole or baked macaroni and cheese, with french fries and potato salad. The faculty dining room was crowded at 12:30, since prime time for classes was the Monday-Wednesday-Friday 11:30 to 12:20 slot.

Glad Gold and Mary Anne Reilly hovered at the salad table, which gave faculty members a vantage point from which to survey the various dining tables and to choose a good one to join. A "good" table was by definition any table which didn't include Irma Freundlich or old Ferenczi (boring, boring, boring) or that new girl in physics who always wanted to talk about how smart she'd been in grad school and college and high school and grade school and nursery school.

"The round one, by the window?" asked Mary Anne, in an undertone. "Mandy Tweedy's there, and Olympia."

"But there are four empty seats," whispered Glad, as she served herself four black olives.

"It's okay," murmured Mary Anne. "Irma and

66

Ferenczi are already sitting down. See the square table near the door?"

"Right," said Glad, taking some potato chips.

The table they joined was occupied by Howard Disher, Mandy Tweedy, Olympia Principe, and old Cabot Coale, and seemed like such an odd assortment that Glad asked, "Is this a committee meeting?" before putting her tray down.

"No; please join us," said Olympia.

After the obligatory first remarks on the starchiness and pale color of the dining hall food, the group moved on to another favorite topic, started by Howard. "The freshmen are different this year. Better."

Glad had been at Turnbull for five years; every year the faculty said the freshmen were better. She thought so, too, every year. Yet, somehow, the quality of the girls, taken as a whole, never seemed to change at all.

"I agree," said silvery old Cabot Coale, who was already on his coffee. "My freshmen are much more diligent. Perhaps even more intelligent."

"And they talk," said Howard. "Sometimes when I ask if there are any questions they actually have some."

"But you know," said Glad, "maybe it's just that freshmen are always better than upperclassmen. What is it we do to kill that enthusiasm? It seems to me the seniors are dull and the freshmen always great, every year."

"Not in the sixties," said Mary Anne Reilly. "Even the seniors were spendid then. We haven't had a class like that since."

"My class was '69," commented Mandy Tweedy proudly.

"My God, that's right," said Olympia. "You were a Turnbull girl, weren't you? And so recently. Disgusting. A baby."

Mandy laughed, pleased.

Cabot, who was lighting his pipe, made a number

of the little kissing sounds that pipe-smokers habitually make, while signaling with his hand that he wished the floor and would speak as soon as he was properly lit. The others waited patiently. "I thought—pup pup—" he said finally, "the class of '69 was execrable. If you ask me we haven't had a really decent bunch since about '57."

"Oh, Cabot, you're a fuddy-duddy," said Mary Anne, without a trace of rancor. "I've been here even longer than you, and I remember the fifties students very well. They were *dull*. The girls of the late sixties may have been foolish and immature sometimes, and their so-called radicalism was never very well thought out, but they cared about ideas. They were . . ."

"They were—pup pup—muddle headed and, what's more—pup—they were the most immoral gang we've ever had."

"Speaking of immorality, Cabot," said Olympia, "I thought your behavior at the candidate sherry yesterday was shocking. I was embarrassed for all of us."

Cabot looked hurt. "I'm surprised, Mrs. Principe, I really am. Don't you share my concern for spiritual values?"

Olympia's enormous dark eyes sparkled with indignation. "Don't you think it's insulting to ask a woman publicly if she plans to have a lover?"

Cabot sucked calmly on his pipe. "No (pup pup) I don't think it's insulting. And these days it's a highly relevant question; after all the lady is a divorcée. . . ."

"And therefore automatically immoral?" asked Olympia angrily.

A hearty voice asked, "Is this a committee meeting?" It was Bruce Longfellow, the Dean of the College.

"No, Bruce, just a fight," said Glad. "Please join us and break it up."

The dean, the number two person at Turnbull, was an attractively ugly man with a big nose, stiff black hair, a red face and a huge untidy moustache. He was a good dean, except for a tendency to push faculty scholarship too hard. He had recently made himself popular with many of the faculty by refusing to be considered for the presidency, on the grounds that the next leader should certainly be a woman.

"I was just leaving," said Cabot, rising. "I have a one o'clock."

"Are we friends?" asked Olympia, with a bright smile on her vivid face.

"Certainly," Cabot said stiffly. "Excuse me."

Bruce Longfellow sat staring at his macaroni and cheese, his potato salad and his creamed onions. "Everything's beige," he said.

"Everything's always beige," said Mandy Tweedy.

"What kind of soup is this?" he asked, staring into the smooth white liquid.

"Cream of flour," said Glad. "Now that Cabot's gone, I have something I want to tell Howard. Are you still collecting vile jokes for Terry's twelfth birthday?"

"Yes," said Howard eagerly. "You got one?"

"I heard this one from Father Bob. Maybe it's in some collection of jokes for sermons or something."

"Keen. That's the sort we need."

"Anyway," said Glad, "this minister gets married. And on the wedding night, the bride waits expectantly for—you know. And nothing happens. Next night, same thing: nothing. Third night, she's beginning to worry. So she asks the minister why no action."

"Those were her precise words?" asked Bruce Longfellow.

"Yes," said Glad firmly. "She says, 'Why no action, Padre?' And he says, gently, 'My dear, it's Lent.' And she says, 'To whom? And for *how long?*'"

"You tell the most refined jokes," said Howard. "They always seem to have 'whom' in them."

"Well, she's a scholar," said the dean affectionately. He liked Glad.

She turned on him. "Publish, publish, publish, that's all you ever think about," she said, partly teasing, partly serious. "Do you know what this man said to me when he interviewed me for the job here?" she asked, turning to Mary Anne.

"No, I don't believe I do."

"I don't remember it myself," admitted Bruce, a slightly uneasy look on his florid face.

"I asked him what people around here do for fun. He said, 'Research.' I said, 'No, I don't think you understood me. Of course faculty members do research in some of their spare time. But when they want to have *fun* in Wading River, what do they do?' And he said, very firmly, 'Research.' Without batting an eye."

"Evil dean," said Howard, smiling. "I've done research and where has it gotten me? Canned."

Bruce looked uncomfortable. "How is the job situation these days, Howie? Any nibbles?"

A look of real anger flashed onto Howard's comfortable cherub face. "Nothing. There are no jobs in my field, except for the very newest, cheapest Ph.D.s. Knight knew that, too. I've sent vitas to more than eighty places. Not one interview."

"God, Howie," said Glad, "what will you do?"

The sudden bitterness left Howard's face, and was replaced by his customary look of resigned good humor. "Barb finally has a speech therapy job at the Middle School. I guess we'll stay here—not on Forsythe Street, of course—and I'll get a job as a night watchman. That way I'll still have lots of time to do—research."

The dean chuckled with embarrassment, then there was a long, awkward silence.

"I've just been named acting president," said Dean

Longfellow. "The Chairman of the Board called me this morning."

"Congratulations," said Mary Anne, echoed by the others.

"I loathe it already," said Bruce cheerily. "Mrs. Pepper's just been filling me in on how many times I have to go out of town this month. I abhor it. Terrified of flying, you know. Like to sleep in my own bed. Hope you presidential search committee guys come up with somebody good soon."

"We're trying," said Glad. "We're on the home-stretch now. Tonight's a big meeting with the trustee committee to narrow the finalists down to two or three."

"The grapevine says it's going to be Lucille Walker England," said Mandy mischievously.

"Oh no you don't," said Mary Anne. "You'll not worm anything out of us that easily."

"It was worth a try," said Howard. "Why does the grapevine choose England, Mandy?"

"Most experience. Lowest voice. Widowed rather than divorced. Said to have contacts with mega-bucks. Doesn't she, Olympia?"

The music professor shook her head and laughed. "Don't tempt me, naughty girl. Besides, I want to ask Bruce something."

The dean wiped cheese sauce off his big moustache. "Yup?"

"Do you know if they've caught the killer yet? Is it safe to walk around the campus at night?"

"Don't know anything about it," said Bruce. "I guess the police guy was around questioning suspects yesterday, but as far as I know nobody's seen him today. Skinny little guy."

"I'm surprised at you, Bruce," said Glad. "That was a vulgar heightist remark."

"The police chief? I thought he was, like, a doll," said Mandy. "Sort of the Dick Cavett type. You want to pat him on the head or something."

"I don't," said Longfellow. "Anyway, we managed to get the newspapers to describe Knight's death as an accidental drowning. Wouldn't want the alums and parents thinking one of us might be a deranged killer."

"But one of us is," said Glad.

Her remark was met with instant and unanimous cries of disagreement. "Oh surely not," said Mary Anne. "It must have been someone from the town, some drug addict or derelict. Mustn't it?"

"Maybe the gang who did the burglaries on Whitaker Street," suggested Howard.

"That was last fall," said Glad. "Why are you all so hasty? Isn't it obvious it's one of us? Who else would pick Knight? Who else could get into the pool? Who else has a motive? It must be one of us or one of our students. I'll bet that at one time or another, every person in this room has said that he or she would like to kill Henderson Knight."

There was a silence. Much sipping of coffee.

Then Olympia said, "I've said it."

"I certainly have, too," admitted Howard. "With good reason. As you all know. But of course I didn't mean it literally." His cherub face looked anxious.

"Well, you know," said Mandy, "I guess I have, too. At least, I've thought it. After he bawled me out in public for wearing blue jeans to the first faculty meeting. Like, in front of the whole faculty? You remember that? I mean, he called me 'young lady,' and everybody turned around and stared at me, and the students in the back, like, laughed and whistled? I guess everybody thought I was too cool to let it faze me, but, you know, it really gets to you, that kind of public thing where everybody laughs. You know what I mean?"

"I remember," said Glad. "I wanted to murder him for that, too."

"Well," said Dean Longfellow, "he had a talent for saying unforgivable things. I could tell you some things—well, as long as we're all rushing to confess, I might as well admit I've had murderous moments with Henderson myself. And I'll bet Mary Anne has, too."

"I'll bet," said Mandy, turning with a smile to the astronomer, "that you wanted to kill him for turning down your sabbatical. Didn't you?"

Mary Anne Reilly's coffee cup rattled noisily as she replaced it in the saucer. She kept staring at the table, not speaking, as if she hadn't heard anything.

Maybe Mary Anne's beginning to go deaf, thought Glad with a wave of sympathy. Sometimes, for a minute or two, she seems the age she really is, or even older. Maybe she just can't bear to think about not getting to Kitt Peak. Poor lady. "About the newspapers," Glad said to Bruce Longfellow, "did we make the *Times?*"

"Page twenty-eight, one paragraph. Page two in the Boston *Globe* this morning, with a picture of him. Nice long write-up. You know, I'd forgotten that Knight used to be such a distinguished scholar. Did you know that his book, *The Age of Millard Fillmore,* won a Tolbert Prize, and a National Book Award?"

"Yeah," said Howard Disher. "It was his dissertation."

"Lucille England's in American history, too," said Mandy.

"Strike against her," said Howard. *"Any* resemblance to Henderson Neville Knight . . ."

Glad chimed in: "The Attleham *Courier-Standard-Star* had a big front page spread right next to the lead article about the tractor-trailer full of water-beds that overturned on 95. The headline read 'Turn-bull Pres. in Mishap: Knight N. Henderson Drowns Fatally.'"

"Like, beautiful," said Mandy. "Trust them to get his names wrong. You know?"

"Is this a meeting?"

Jack Witherspoon had approached the table with an eye on Cabot Coale's vacated chair.

The diners urged the art historian to join them. Some greeted him with almost excessive cordiality.

Bruce Longfellow was particularly hearty; by this, Witherspoon understood instantly that even the dean knew about his Shocking Problem.

"Say," said Glad, "I've got a question for all of you."

"God!" said Jack, regarding his lunch. "Macaroni and potatoes with my noodles. How low can they sink?"

"Wait till you get to the rice pudding," suggested Mary Anne.

"And it's all beige," said Longfellow.

"It's *always* all beige," said Mandy. "But, like, what was your question, Glad?"

"Have any of you received an anonymous letter lately? Student handwriting and spelling, written in brown ink?"

The other teachers shook their heads. After a pause Howard Disher said, "I guess you must have, huh? What about, Glad?"

"Accusing another student of cheating. Not giving any evidence, though, just an accusation."

"That's really disturbing," said Mary Anne sympathetically. "If a girl's going to turn in a fellow student—and I don't mean to say she shouldn't, necessarily—she should have the courage to make her accusation openly. What are you going to do about it?"

Glad was lighting a cigarette. "I—I'm going to think about it. It was supposedly a plagiarized paper, and I've returned all the papers already. I don't think it's true: the paper wasn't all that good; I remember it pretty well. But I guess I'll have to check the bibliography on the next one pretty carefully."

The student waitress came to their table to refill coffee cups, so they discreetly changed the subject.

A few minutes later, Glad excused herself, and left the dining room. She went across the faculty lounge to the coat room, put on her jacket and was picking up her briefcase when Olympia Principe came hurrying across the lounge. "Wait a minute, Glad," said the dark-eyed musician, in an urgent but soft voice.

"Yes?"

"I didn't want to say anything in front of Jack or the dean, but I got one of those brown-ink poison-pen jobs."

"Oh really?" Glad put down her heavy briefcase. "Accusing a student of cheating?"

Olympia shook her dark head. "No. Accusing Jack Witherspoon. Of using the piano practice rooms in Kola Hall for clandestine assignations with students. The practice rooms are almost soundproof, you know. Makes a logical place. The Oliviero Memorial Room—the one with the harpsichord—even has a couch."

"Oh boy," said Glad, with a worried frown. "Did the note say clandestine assignations?"

"No, actually it said 'balling.' "

"Oh, wow. The note I got accused C.C. Duxbury."

"Ohmigod," whispered Olympia. "That's Jack's little girl friend, right? The pretty Oceanid in the grotesque baseball chest-protector?"

"Right. Looks as if we've got a kind of a sick student on our hands."

"Should we tell Mandy Tweedy? That would be in her domain, wouldn't it? And in spite of her sixties jargon, she actually handles the kids with a lot of common sense."

Glad frowned. "I guess we should tell her. But first let's see if we can figure out who Ms. Poison Pen is."

Olympia nodded. Two biologists entered the coat room from outdoors. Glad again picked up her heavy briefcase.

"Who's driving to the search committee meeting tonight?" she asked.

"My turn," said Olympia. "Pick you up at ten of five?"

Glad's heart sank. Olympia's driving displayed a creative style which always left Glad exhausted with tension. "Fine," she said. "Hi, Mabel. Hi, Frieda," she said to the biologists.

"Have you seen the *Courier-Standard-Star* today?" asked Frieda. "Just came out. Look at that."

The biologist held up the Attleham paper, so they could read the headline.

ARREST IN SLAYING OF EDUCATER the headline screamed. The subhead read: SECURITY GAURD CHARGED.

"How appalling!" said Glad. *"Two* misspellings in one headline."

Chapter Eight

March 16: 4:10 p.m.

ACTING CHIEF Alden Chase was depressed. He sat in his office and chewed pencils.

He tried turning on the radio, which he kept tuned to his favorite Boston station. Sometimes, if the music was right, it helped him to think. There was nothing so relaxing as a nice catchy hummable tune, or a good steady beat. Baroque was his favorite period; he particularly liked Scarlatti.

This music wasn't right. Random notes, random rhythm, unidentifiable instruments. Electronic. Chase switched it off fast, and went to his bookshelf. He took out Sygoda's *Law of Manslaughter and Homicide* and sat down to read.

After five minutes he marked his place, closed the book, and returned it to the shelf.

Goddamnit, he thought. Maybe I'm turning into a fruitcake like Professor Witherspoon. Maybe I need the air conditioner humming.

No, I don't.

What I need is to get those goddamn selectmen off my back.

He spat a fragment of pencil wood into the clean glass ashtray on his desk.

I also need to start smoking again.

No! He was horrified at himself. I don't need a cigarette; I don't even want one. I need to feel sure that

Nick Fowler killed Henderson Knight, that's what I need.

The three selectmen—Collins, Rizzio and Dupont—had been hanging around the station the day before, pumping Patrolwoman Donnelly about the murder, when Al Shirley brought in Nick Fowler, who seemed like a confused old alcoholic. Right in front of Fowler, Collins blurted out, "You gonna chahge im for murdrin Hendason Knight, ahnt you, Chief?"

Tight-lipped, Chase had rushed Fowler down to the gleaming new lockup, but the damage had already been done: Fowler was stumbling and trembling and saying, "I din't kill nobody," and "Has Present Knight been killed?" all the way to the cell. By the time Chase had evicted the selectmen and got back to Fowler, it was impossible to get anything straight out of him. He acted extremely surprised about Knight's death and extremely indignant about being detained. The surprise and the indignation were certainly exaggerated. But was it totally phony, or was the overacting due to Fowler's understandable and obviously real terror? Thanks to Selectman Collins, it was impossible to tell, and within minutes the frightened old rummy was refusing to say more without a lawyer.

His rights, of course. Chase, unlike many of his colleagues, did not regard the Supreme Court as a worse enemy than the Mafia. He definitely regarded the Mafia as worse. He had taken a night course on constitutional law at Jennings College, and had come to see that the Supreme Court performed an irritating but necessary function, like the I.R.S., or the umpires at Red Sox games. Or, maybe, like the forest fires that thin forests beneficially. Or the predator animals that weed out the unhealthy deer. Or the mosquitoes that—what hidden good do mosquitoes do?

Chase's ex-wife had been very ecology-minded; he

was sure she'd have some explanation for why it was foolish and wrong to kill mosquitoes, but he couldn't at the moment think of any.

Anyway, not only had Selectman Collins spoiled Fowler for him, he'd also called an emergency meeting in the selectmen's office that night—last night. At which all three selectmen had told Acting Chief Chase that if he wanted to remain acting chief very long, he'd better act now, and charge Fowler immediately with murder.

"But Knight hasn't even been dead twenty-four hours," protested Chase. "Can't you give me a little time? I'm not really sure Fowler did it."

"Aw, come on Alden, sure he did it. Tried to skip town, didn't he?" asked Collins.

"We sure as hell don't have the evidence for a conviction," insisted Chase, "and he sure as hell isn't in any confessing mood."

"Well, then," said Selectman Dupont, chewing on his little cigar, "you sure as hell better get him into a confessing mood. I don't mean nothing illegal, of course. . . ."

"Make him a deal," suggested Rizzio. "You know, some of that stuff they did with Spiro Agnew, whatchacallit bargaining?"

"Plea bargaining?" asked Chase.

"Yeah. That's the stuff. Please-bargaining. Wrap it up quick. We don't want the citizens of Wading River thinking there's some psycho killer wandering around at large, do we? I've been getting a lot of scared phone calls."

"Me, too," said Collins. "I hardly got any plumbing calls all day, nothing but this murder business every time the phone rang. Beats me how news travels so fast, even in a big town like Wading River. And I'm up for re-election this year, you know."

"Yeah," said Chase. "So you want me to plea bargain. I guess I'll have to call Judge Dorman and talk to him. Are you planning to have me prosecute?"

"Sure, why not?" said Rizzio, shrugging his shoulders. "You got a pretty good track record."

Chase was surprised; it was the first word of praise he'd ever had from a selectman. He did have a good track record; he'd only lost two cases all last year. "Thanks," he said somewhat uneasily, "but those were mostly small stuff, you know. Routine B & E, lewd and lascivious speech and behavior, driving to endanger, possession of class A substance, stuff like that. This is murder. I figured you'd want to bring somebody in from outside to investigate, to say nothing of the trial stuff. We'll have to have a jury, you know, for a capital crime. I've never faced anybody but Judge Dorman and Judge Polese. Hell, you know I'm not a lawyer."

Selectman Dupont stubbed out his cigar. He was tired of the conversation, and wanted to go home. He had to get up early in the morning; he was a deliveryman for Heer Dairy. "Well, Alden," he said jovially, "I guess you better study up for it."

"Wait a minute," said Rizzio. "We're not gonna stick the citizens of Wading River for a jury trial, are we? I mean, that would cost money. We don't have no money in the budget for juries and prosecutors and all that crap."

"We'd have to have a special town meeting and request the money," said Collins.

"We'd never get a quorum," said Dupont pessimistically. "We don't even get a quorum when it's something hot like a school bond issue." All three magistrates shook their heads gloomily.

"Well, what do you want me to do?" asked Chase, with barely restrained irritation, "let Fowler go and forget the whole thing?"

"That would be nice," said Dupont. "Do you think we can do that?"

"I don't think so," said Collins thoughtfully. "I think Alden here should really hit those books. He should dream up some charge Fowler will agree to, where we won't need a jury. But something where we can sock Fowler away for a good long time. After all, we want to think a little about justice, don't we?"

The other selectmen agreed solemnly that Collins's plan seemed good to them. Acting Chief Chase was permitted to leave. The selectmen went home to bed.

So here was Chase, only one day after the murder of Henderson Knight, sitting at his desk, chewing pencils and wondering whether Nick Fowler, who had been arraigned that morning, was guilty after all.

It seemed likely. Life wasn't, after all, like the detective novels; usually the likeliest suspect was in fact the right one to collar. Fowler was a kind of pathetic old lush; Chase would have preferred to nab one of those high-and-mighty professors, or one of those luscious rich college girls. But, statistically, college professors and beautiful girls don't really commit many murders; mostly, they read about them.

Fowler had a good motive; he had a key to the pool; he had tried to leave town. But—

The phone rang. Al, at the main desk, called out: "It's a lady, wants to speak to you, named Gold, line one."

"I'll take it."

Chase's thin shoulders straightened automatically; he sat up taller and put down his mangled pencil.

Her voice on the phone was low and melodious. "I hope I'm not disturbing you," said Glad. "Were you brushing your teeth or anything?"

He laughed. His first laugh of the day. "I'm in my office," he said. "But I'll switch the call to the john if you'd like, so you can hear what the shower sounds like."

"Oh goody. Listen, Chief Chase, I really think you made a mistake in arresting Nick Fowler."

"Oh? Why do you say that?"

"I know Nick pretty well, and he's a really sweet old man. He wouldn't have killed Prexy for firing him; Nick expected to be fired. He knew he wasn't doing his job properly; he told me so himself one night last week. I was in my office working late and he came by on his rounds. He had been scared to death when he saw the light in my office, he said. He was obviously half-crocked, and he poured out a long confession about his sad life and his wicked drinking habit and about how he expected to lose this job pretty soon, the way he'd lost all his other jobs. Honestly, Chief, I think you've got the wrong man."

Chase was frowning, but felt a small surge of relief.

"You might just be right," he said. "But, well—that's unprofessional of me to say. I hope you won't repeat it."

"I promise," she said. "Are you glad I called? I mean, was that helpful, what I just told you?"

"Yes," he said.

"Can I talk to you some more?" she asked. "I mean about other possible suspects? Now that it's a matter of helping poor Nick, I might be able to work harder at thinking of other relevant details."

Chase smiled. "Good. That would be helpful. Maybe—would you—if you're free for dinner tonight?"

There was a little pause. "Dammit," said the melodious voice, "I'm not free. I have to go to a meeting in Boston. We may be choosing the new president tonight."

"Oh well," he said casually, "it wouldn't have been a really good time for me either."

"How about lunch tomorrow?" she asked brightly. "I'm free from twelve twenty-five on."

"Fine," said Chase. "I'll pick you up in your office."

She hung up. Chase took out a fresh pencil, and switched on his radio. It was some Bach piece, for un-accompanied violin. "Now there," he said to himself with satisfaction, "is a tune you can whistle."

Chapter Nine

March 16: 5:20 p.m.

MARY ANNE REILLY was in the back seat of Olympia's car; it was better for her slipped disc because she could put her legs up. Glad, therefore, sat in the front, in a better position to observe Olympia's creative spontaneity as a driver. She found that by fixing her eyes directly on Olympia's lovely face, she could refrain, most of the time, from giving irritating warnings about red lights and upcoming turns; she was also less likely to flinch, or to slam her long legs down on imaginary brakes at Olympia's near-misses of other cars.

As they rode, the women were planning their strategy for the search committee meeting.

"Frankly," said Mary Anne a little wearily, "I'd be perfectly willing to vote for Rosen, England, *or* Day. I must admit England seems the most presidential to me, but that might just be because she's the oldest. I could accept any of those three."

"But what about Mr. Williams?" asked Glad. "Don't you suppose that's who the trustees secretly want?"

"No, I really don't think so," said Mary Anne firmly. "I think we have to accept as sincere their statement last fall, when they agreed with us it should be a woman, if possible."

"I don't trust Palmer Jordan on that," said Olympia, twisting almost all the way around, to make sure Mary Anne heard her. The big Chrysler swerved halfway out of the middle lane. Glad felt a rush of adrenaline, but she controlled herself and merely widened her eyes; Olympia calmly pulled the car back between the white lines. They were still far from Boston; the traffic on route 95 was still fortunately sparse. Thank God, it's a big vulgar car, thought Glad, and not a VW like mine. Maybe we'll only be maimed. Then again, if we're killed, it will free up three tenure slots.

"I know," said Mary Anne, "but you must admit Palmer's restrained himself pretty much so far."

Palmer Jordan was the most conservative trustee on their committee. He was a big, red-faced, beautifully dressed manufacturer of quality hairbrushes—a man whose influence upon the board seemed rather out of proportion to his apparent intelligence. His wife and four daughters were all enthusiastic Turnbull alumnae; he was rumored to be rich enough to support the school out of his back pocket. But maybe his power over the board came simply from sheer arrogance, an unquestioning assumption that his opinion counted for more than other people's. The other trustee members of the search committee, though it would be wrong to characterize them as flaming radicals, were all bright people, not at all the bloated barbarians the faculty members had expected them to be. Jane Della Rosa, their celebrated journalist alum, was a tough lady and a delight; Winston Wulff, a banker, was good-natured and sensible; and Bill Schuster, an elderly lawyer, was courtly, amusing and a tactful mediator. The meetings, so far, had been fun, and no major conflicts had developed.

In narrowing down the candidates to six finalists, they had gone through hundreds of vitas and drunk quarts of coffee together, and had gotten to know each other pretty well. Personal prejudices had emerged, but none seemed particularly sinister. It became a standing joke that Bill Schuster, the oldest committee member, was consistently opposed to any candidate over 50 years old; Glad was against anyone with an education degree; Jane Della Rosa mistrusted Southerners; Winston Wulff disliked ministers. The group came to laugh at each individual's quirks, and to discount them almost automatically. They had not really had much trouble arriving at fourteen semi-finalists, and when they had interviewed these, there had still been no serious disagreement about which six should be invited to the campus for the full treatment. At least, there had been no trustee-faculty divisions.

"Tonight," said Glad, "is the crunch. Now we'll find out whether this era of good feeling is real. I think we ought to agree on our choices, and present a united front; if we aren't agreed, Palmer Jordan might just force Williams on us."

"Oh no," said Mary Anne, horrified. "We can't allow that. I think we'll have to say that the one candidate we find totally unacceptable is Williams."

"But," said Glad, lighting a cigarette, "what if they ask us about the opinion of the rest of the faculty? Remember, after those sherry free-for-alls most of the men and even some of the women thought Williams was at least second best, if not first. And they were in total disagreement about the women."

"Williams is a smoothie, all right," admitted Mary Anne. "As far as his vita's concerned, he looks ideal. He has everything: deaning experience, scholarly publication, grantsmanship, happy little family, nice voice, a dazzling smile. He even looks like a college president."

"He's even gray at the temples," said Glad.

"Central casting," said Olympia, "just like our late lamented."

"I agree," said Glad, "and so does Jane Della Rosa, obviously. And Muffy Work tells me the students

loathed Williams. But what if we can't agree on one
of the women? Honestly, Olympia, which would you
like best?"

"Day. Or Rosen. Maybe Rosen best. But I don't
think we'll convince the trustees. They'd never admit they were anti-Semitic, but . . . "

Glad exhaled smoke. "I know. In fact, I don't think
they think they are. They'll probably just say she
isn't the Turnbull type. They'll insist she'd be better
suited to a city university. Maybe they'd go so far as
to mention her accent—*Olympia!*"

Screech. Beep beep.

Olympia had changed lanes impulsively, thereby
enraging several drivers, one of whom now roared
past the Chrysler with his middle finger up. Olympia smiled brightly, and flicked her chin at him with
Italian nonchalance. Glad inhaled deeply.

"I'm for Diane Day," she said. "But I agree with
Mary Anne; I could go for Rosen, Day or England,
whichever the trustees will support."

"I think they'll go for England," suggested Mary
Anne. "She's the most mature. The most experi-
enced. Perhaps less imaginative . . . "

"Yes," said Glad, "I agree. Do you like her best?"

The astronomy professor answered slowly, with
care, "No—I don't like her best. Rosen seems to me
the brightest. And I like Day immensely: she seems
sharp, open, vigorous—and I don't object to her
youth. But Lucille England seems the safest. I feel
confident that she wouldn't be a disaster. The others
just might be."

"True," said Olympia. "Actually, it's amazing to
me that here we are, almost ready for the final vote.
How little we really know these candidates."

"We know they've performed well where they've
been before," said Glad. "We know they handle
themselves well in interviews. We know they are
well educated; we know they have admirers willing

to write enthusiastic recommendations for them. I'm ready to vote: one two three, Day, Rosen, England."

"I'd go Rosen, Day, England," said Olympia.

"And I'd make it England, Day, Rosen," laughed Mary Anne.

"Olympia . . ." began Glad, gently and tentatively.

"Yes?"

"Isn't our exit coming up pretty soon?"

Beep beep *honk*. Glad's word was as good as a command, for the big Chrysler lurched in front of a bus, across two lanes and bumped on and off the shoulder.

Mary Anne moaned softly.

"Sorry," said Olympia contritely, "I forgot about your back. Are you all right, Mary Anne?"

"My back's all right," said Mary Anne, "but my few remaining brown hairs just went white. I was hoping they'd hold out till my retirement party."

"I really am sorry," said the musician humbly. "I'll try to pay more attention to the driving. Oops, here's our turn!"

Glad and Mary Anne braced themselves for the exciting trip down the spiraling off-ramp.

The meeting was to be in one of the executive dining rooms at Winston Wulff's bank. One of the fringe benefits of this search, for the faculty women, had been the quiet little sumptuous dinners at various trustee hangouts, where the service was fast and unobtrusive, the food simple but of fine quality, and the menus never mentioned M-O-N-E-Y. At the first meeting Glad had been so childishly dazzled by the thought that it was all free that she had greedily consumed two cocktails and wine and shrimp and broiled tenderloin with mushrooms and baked potato with sour cream and salad and hot butterscotch rolls and strawberry shortcake. In time, however, she became accustomed to the rich and powerful atmosphere of the private dining rooms, and admitted to herself that two drinks plus wine made her talk a little funny and that all that food made her waistband uncomfortable. So she had learned to settle for one cocktail and wine plus shrimp plus tenderloin and potato and peach melba. Ah well, it would all be over soon. A good thing, really. Since the search had begun, Glad had done no work on her Tennyson book, which she loved writing, and for which she had a contract with Harvard Press.

As Olympia pulled into the parking lot, the professors finally came to a hasty agreement. They would go for any of the three women finalists who seemed to attract a majority of trustees, but if there was no agreement and it looked as though Williams were a threat, they would vote in a bloc for Diane Day.

They met Jane Della Rosa in the ladies' room on the executive dining room floor. Olympia was brushing her cloud of glossy black hair; Mary Anne was putting hairpins into her untidy gray bun; Glad was trying, for the third time, to wash the shoe polish stains off her fingers.

"That's what I get," she said, "for trying to ape me betters. I wanted my shoes to be as shiny as Palmer Jordan's; I end up with navy blue cuticles."

"I love your pantsuit," said Jane Della Rosa, admiring Glad's red corduroys. Jane herself looked, as usual, like the chairman of the Keokuk Eastern Star bake sale, with her tight permanent and pearls.

"Oh thank you! You know, I never know whether to wear a skirt and try to disarm the male trustees and gain their confidence, or to wear my usual comfy pants and maybe antagonize them."

Miss Della Rosa laughed as she powdered her large nose. "You might as well wear the pants and the hell with them," she said. "They'd know you're not one of them even if you wore mink. They want you to be an egghead liberal and libber; that's your role. You play yours; they play theirs. They like it that way, and they like you fine. You know, they actually respect you professors, even fear you a little.

In spite of their contempt for your innocence and poverty—maybe because of it. Like priests, you know. Most Catholics wouldn't want to be priests, but voluntary chastity is heavy—gives the priest a hell of a lot of power."

"That's all very well," said Mary Anne severely, "but do they respect our opinions enough to support a woman president?"

"Palmer Jordan won't," said the newspaperwoman firmly. "The old bastard's really quaking in his boots about the idea. You know what he whispered to old Bill Schuster after the interview with Williams?"

The three professors quickly gathered around Jane's mirror. "What did he say?" asked Mary Anne, eagerly, in a hushed voice.

" 'That's our man,' " said Jane angrily. "How do you like that? Not even 'that's our new president,' just 'our man.' "

"What can we do?" asked Olympia, worried.

Jane Della Rosa scowled. "Fight the bastard," she said loudly. "Schuster and Wulff are probably all right, maybe a little bewildered. But Palmer Jordan still thinks we should use the Old Boy system. You know, he was on the search committee that chose Henderson Knight ten years ago. So you know how many candidates were considered in that search? About five. All nominated by academic cronies of the trustees. Needless to say, all Ivy, and all male."

"I've seen the files from that search," said Olympia. "You're right. Maybe twenty or thirty nominations came in, from alumnae, faculty and so on, but the committee only considered a handful. In fact, Mary Anne Reilly was one of those nominated. Were you ever interviewed, Mary Anne?"

The astronomer smiled modestly; it was possible to see, on her plump lined face, for a moment, traces of that beauty which all the old guard at Turnbull remembered fondly. "I heard some time later that I'd been nominated," she said in her precise, soft voice. "But I was never even contacted by the committee."

"That's appalling," said Glad.

"Oh no." Mary Anne smiled. "I wouldn't have wanted the job anyway. What sane person would? I'm a teacher and an astronomer, not a fund-raiser or glad-hander."

"You're a peach," said Olympia, hugging Mary Anne impulsively. Mary Anne looked acutely uncomfortable. "Shouldn't we go and join the gentlemen?" she suggested.

Glad's cords went wip-wip-wip as she walked down the hall.

The three men were drinking already. The atmosphere was one of jovial tension.

Winston Wulff was just finishing a joke. "So you know what they've decided to call a mailman?" he asked. "A person-person."

After the laugh subsided, Jane Della Rosa said, "I can't imagine what subject you guys were discussing before we came."

There was another round of laughter. Then, Bill Schuster, the elderly lawyer who was chairman of the committee, asked them to sit down with their cocktails so the meeting could begin.

It was quickly agreed that two of the six finalists were no longer in the running, one man because he bored everyone to tears, one woman because she obviously didn't want the job and didn't have a kind word to say about any aspect of Turnbull.

"That," said Schuster, "leaves Mrs. Day, Miss Rosen, Mrs. England and Mr. Williams. Can we eliminate any of them immediately?"

"As far as I'm concerned," said Jane Della Rosa in her loud voice, "you can leave out Williams."

"Now wait a minute," put in Palmer Jordan, red-faced from his two martinis. "Aren't you just saying that because he's a man? The bottom line is that he's the only candidate we've got with any financial

know-how. In fact, he's the only one who comes any-
where near the level not only of Henderson Knight—
rest his soul—but any of the candidates we saw last
time around."

Wulff, who was usually the quietest member of the
group, said softly, "I thought he was slippery."

"Hooray," said Glad, "I'm happy someone else
saw it. Nothing he said had anything to do with
Turnbull; you couldn't pin him down on anything. It
was all fine phrases, selling himself."

"I agree," said Olympia, "it was always on the one
hand this, on the other hand that. No content."

"But," said Schuster judiciously, "shouldn't a college president be a bit of a politician, really? He
certainly has a number of constituencies whose in-
terests are often opposed. Students, faculty, alumnae, parents, trustees, the public—"

"But this man," protested Mary Anne, "seemed to
have no principles at all. Now Mrs. England, for example, was tactful, but you knew where she stood on
several key issues."

"Is it fair for me to conclude," asked Bill Schuster
gently, "that the general feeling is opposed to Mr.
Williams?"

"Let's not count him out yet," said Jordan angrily.

"All right," said Schuster in an amiable voice.
"What about Mrs. Rosen?"

Palmer Jordan turned his thumbs down. "Not the
Turnbull type," he said. "The accent alone . . . "

Olympia snorted. "You're going to eliminate her
just because of her accent?" she asked. (She hadn't
quite said "justa because-a," but a distinctly Italian-
ate tone had suddenly graced Olympia's words.)

"Well frankly," said Winston Wulff, "I felt she
might be better suited to an urban university. She
seemed so . . . aggressive."

"And that haircut," Jordan reminded them, his
face almost purple against his white hair.

"Would you be interested in a trade?" suggested Glad, with her most dimpled smile.

"How do you mean?"

"Rosen for Williams. Eliminate them both."

Jordan swallowed a gulp of martini. "Maybe," he said.

Bill Schuster polled the other committee members. They were all agreeable to the choice of either Day or England. Glad, Olympia and Winston Wulff were for Diane Day; Mary Anne, Bill Schuster and Jane Della Rosa supported Lucille England. Palmer Jordan called a plague on both their houses.

"I must admit," said Mary Anne, "that I would like to know more about Mrs. Day. I don't consider her impossible. I might be persuaded to switch my vote."

"I feel the same way about Lucille England," said Wulff. "And we don't, of course, know for sure that any of these candidates will accept the position in the final analysis."

"There's another thing," said Glad. "All the letters we've read about these people are from their supporters, so of course they're favorable. But I don't think we've dug quite enough to find their enemies. They must have them. We've done some calling, but maybe not enough."

"I agree," said Bill Schuster. "What would you say to an intensive telephone campaign to find enemies of Day and England? Not just at the places they now work, but places they've been in the past?"

The committee agreed wearily that it was a good idea.

"All right," said the old lawyer happily. "Let's divide up the chores. And what would you think of having one more dinner for each of them, at which we'd ask each to give a little speech about what she would do for the college?"

"Great," said Mary Anne.

Jane Della Rosa grumbled about having to fly up from New York again, but agreed.

The others agreed.

"Well," said Palmer Jordan finally, "at least Mrs. England and Mrs. Day are both ladies."

Glad was given as her assignment the job of finding out more about the two women as graduate students. Mary Anne was to look up their publications and find out several scholars' opinions on their merits. Everyone else got a similar chore, to be completed as rapidly as possible.

Dinner was excellent, as usual. Glad allowed herself strawberry shortcake.

After the meeting, Glad, Mary Anne and Olympia left the bank building. They maintained a discreet silence until they were inside the big Chrysler with the doors shut.

Then Olympia whooped, "Hooray!" and Glad laughed, saying "We've won!" and Mary Anne smiled broadly. "The beginning of a new era for Turnbull," she said. "Whichever one it is, it won't be another Henderson Knight. The king is dead; long live the queen!"

Her wrinkled face looked lovely. But the thought of the murdered king was sobering. They fell silent, and remained so almost until route 95.

It was late at night, but Mrs. Pepper was still typing. Polly, as President Knight's executive secretary, had in her office in Shaw Hall most of the college's secret files. And she alone—as the high priestess and guardian of Knight's thoughts—had the key to his last decisions. On his last day the president had given Polly many important things to type: His final report to the trustees. The discussions from his last recorded tapes. The discussion with a concerned student. Rather heated discussion with Mary Anne Reilly—sabbatical denied. Charlene Christiansen: the elimination of her department perhaps. England, a candidate for Knight's job. The drunken security guard. Irma Freundlich—about Disher. Memo to send to college lawyer, *re* Witherspoon, Duxbury. Letter to recommend a grant for Gold to be sent to the Helmreich Foundation. Memo to the chaplain.

She was tired. Her back was hurting, as usual. Her neck and shoulders—tight strings, ready to break. Headache, too. Tensions. But now, thank God, finished.

Hurray. All done.

Mrs. Pepper put all of the beautifully typed reports, memos, letters, minutes into her lockable desk drawer and locked it.

Now she had time to cry. She couldn't stop it. It went on and on. No more memos, no more letters, no more reports, no more splendid speeches.

No more Henderson.

I'm exhausted. I've been such a good woman. I've been almost too good. A martyr?

Oh God, God, God. Everything he told me to do, I did it. I never complained. Stupid. Why? What did he give me, actually? Life stinks.

She stopped crying. Felt a little better. He was only a person, after all. No God.

I can make my back feel better by swimming; then I can go home and have a good stiff drink.

She put on her coat, locked her office and left the building. She started walking to the Pearce Building.

Oh Lord. What an idiot.

I do everything so automatically I don't even think where I'm walking. Lordy, Lordy. I've been going to the place where he died. Just because my hurting back takes me to the pool without letting my mind do anything.

Then again . . . he is dead, and I'm alive. And I want my back to stop hurting, and it wouldn't hurt him, would it? Goddamnit, I'm strong enough to go there and swim if I want to . . . and not even think about him. It's for me and my back.

She had a pool key, of course. She went in, opened her locker, put on her attractive bathing suit and one of the Oceanid's bathing caps.

The water was glorious. All her muscles relaxed. She even began to smile. I'm still young enough to swim well, and fast, too. I still have tone enough to have good-looking legs. I'm not a bag of bones; I'm still an attractive woman.

What's going on? Oh no! God no!

Someone had turned the lights off. It was totally dark.

"Who's there?" she screamed loudly. "Is it a guard? Turn the lights back on, right now; I'm in the pool! *Who is it?*"

Fear. Instant fear. She was a strong swimmer, but to be in the water, in deep water, when it is completely suddenly dark is frightening all by itself . . . and she heard footsteps, probably masculine, heavy. Not too far from the shallow end of the pool. Then they stopped.

Does he want to find me?

Does he want to drown me?

I know too much.

Is this the one who killed Henderson?

Which of them?

Oh God, oh God.

She was treading in the middle of the pool. The footsteps were silent.

Where is he now? What can I do? If I get out of the pool he'll hear me. Can I stay in the pool all night? Will he stay?

There was a sudden loud splash. Oh God, he's in the pool! He must have taken off his shoes. I've got to get out.

She heard the sound of that unseen body gliding toward her. She swam as fast as she could to the side, pulled herself up and out—knew she couldn't run on the wet pavement for fear of slipping. She was panting. He must hear me. She started walking a few steps, then stopping to listen. No sound.

He must still be in the pool. Could be gliding silently to one of the sides. Can he hear me? I can't hear him.

She tiptoed to the spectators' door. Then walked faster out of the lobby. Out of the building. Left her clothes and coat and purse in the building. Ran to her own house, her empty little house so close to the campus. She locked the front door. All the windows. Oh God, I'm still alive. Frozen. Bare feet, wet bathing suit, chilly night, maybe thirty-five degrees? I'm exhausted, too.

But, oh God . . . alive.

Then again, what a fool I was. I didn't wait outside of the building to see who he is.

Who wants to kill me?

Chapter Ten

March 17: 9:30 a.m.

PEOPLE AT TURNBULL were surprised when they realized that Mrs. Pepper wasn't at work.

"She's not at home, either," said Rowena to Mandy.

"Oh well," said Mandy, "that means she isn't sick, at least. You know, I think, she's never had a single sick day for ten years."

Then they both thought of the same appalling idea at the same time. "We'd better get one of the guards to look in her house, right now," said Rowe.

"Shit, yes."

Then Mandy called Mrs. Knight. That was a great relief: Polly had called Melanie early in the morning. "Polly's having a vacation for the first time in a long time," Mandy reported. "She said she'd finished all the typing she had to do for him last night. Since she's done her—you know—duty and is pretty depressed, I imagine, she decided to split for a while. Like for a few weeks or so. And she's not going to tell anybody where she's going. Far out, right?"

Ms. Jackson agreed. "I hope she's in Florida already, getting tanned."

Muffy Work was in Glad's office getting a rundown on the big search committee meeting of the night before. Muffy hadn't been invited to the Boston meeting, but she and Annette Gosling, the other student member of the committee, had met all six finalists, had led them on campus tours and entertained them at lunch with larger groups of students.

It was torture for Muffy to sit and listen to Professor Gold. Muffy was the sort of youngster invariably described as "bouncy" or "bubbly"; it was difficult to bounce and bubble while sitting still. She did manage to nod a lot while she listened—that made her blond curls jiggle attractively—but she was relieved when the briefing was over.

"Golly, Professor Gold," she bubbled, "it sounds like a super meeting. I mean, I wish I'd been there!"

"Well, you and Annette are invited to the final dinners for Day and England."

"Oh, wow!" cried the student, bouncing a little in her chair. "How exciting! I just love meeting with the trustees!"

Glad smiled warmly, but her long legs unconsciously inched her swivel chair back a trifle, further away from Muffy. Muffy's enthusiasm was often termed infectious and Glad had an instinctive aversion to catching it.

Muffy sensed that the meeting was over and bounced to her feet. "Now, Professor Gold," she said, in her friendliest campus pol voice, "I want you to be real sure and tell me if there's anything I can do to help you, you hear? I mean, in your investigations about Day and England?"

"Thanks, Muffy," said Glad. "I'll be sure to remember that. But the main thing you and Annette can do is to use every discretion about who the finalists are. The trustees were very insistent about that, you know."

Muffy looked insulted for a quick moment, then jiggled her curls vigorously and seriously. "Oh, I know," she said with great earnestness. "I won't breathe a word, to anybody, of course. Some of the girls would blab it all over campus: you really can't trust most undergraduates, you know. That's why we have to have rules. And I hate to say it, but there are even some professors around here you can't trust. If you know what I mean."

Glad nodded uneasily. Muffy started to wiggle into her foxfur sweater. Glad herself rose; it was almost time for her eleven o'clock Victorian lit class.

"Well, take care," said Muffy with casual intimacy, as she picked up her green and pink canvas book bag.

"Goodbye, Muffy."

Glad tucked a Browning into her own briefcase and stood for a moment, thinking. She went to the door of her office. "Oh, wait a minute, Muffy," she called. Muffy had already bounced halfway down the hall, but she turned and came back.

"What can I do for you?" she inquired, smiling.

"You can do me a big favor," said Glad.

"Oh, anything," said Muffy, quivering with helpfulness.

"I'm in a really big hurry," said Glad as she buttoned her coat, "and I have to leave an important note for Professor Coale. Could you write one for me, and thumbtack it to my door? Just say 'Professor Coale: I won't be able to meet you for lunch today.' Can you do that for me? I'm in such a hurry. Have you got a pen?"

"Oh, sure I do," said Muffy. "Don't worry about a thing. You run along now, Professor Gold."

"Thanks a million!"

Glad half ran out of the Dahl building then slowed down. Actually she had another eight minutes to do the two-minute walk to her class.

She ducked around the back side of Dahl and reentered through the basement door. Then she paused for several minutes in the hall, outside the office of one of the economics people. Students hurried past her on their way to 11 o'clocks. She read the notices on the econ bulletin board: they were mostly posters advertising MBA programs, but there were a few cartoons about economists. Not very funny.

She looked at her watch; it was 10:59. Well, her students could wait; she had to retrieve the note, in case Cabot should see it and be astonished. Muffy must have left by now.

Glad went up the back stairs to her office. Muffy was gone; there was the note.

Excitedly, Glad ripped the paper from the message board, went into her office, and closed the door. The anonymous accusation was in her briefcase; she put the two notes side by side on her desk.

"Dear Proffessor Gold," said one. "Dear Proffessor Coale," went the other. The first had been written with a brown felt-tip pen. The second had been written with a purple felt-tip pen. The first was written in an affected, ornate handwriting; the second was printed.

Damn.

It wasn't conclusive. Half the students used felt-tip pens; almost as many misspelled professor.

Damn.

Glad went to Victorian lit. It was a lovely group this year, eleven good kids who liked to talk, who responded to imagery, who laughed at Glad's jokes, and who were even mildly interested in prosody.

Today was Browning. Glad told them what Oscar Wilde had said: "Meredith is a prose Browning." Dutifully, the students wrote it down in their notebooks. "And so is Browning." Some of them wrote that in the notebooks, too, but most laughed.

C.C. Duxbury was there, beautiful as ever but rather subdued. She hardly spoke during the 80 minutes of the class. It was a good class, too, a good fight about the merits of *Childe Roland to the Dark Tower Came.*

After class, Glad stopped C.C. She waited, a little nervously, till the other students had left the classroom. "Listen," she said finally, "I've been meaning

to speak to you, Cecilia. Something very disturbing
has been said to me about you, and I wonder if we
could get it cleared up."

C.C.'s large blue eyes filled with tears. "Oh, Miss
Gold," she said huskily, "it's simply awful! I didn't
know you knew."

Glad was embarrassed by the emotion. She felt
that she ought to put a hand on the child's shoulder
or something; wouldn't that be the right human ges-
ture? But she couldn't bring herself to cross the distance; instead, she fished a Kleenex from her purse
and handed it to the student. "I wasn't sure," she
said. "I'd already handed it back to you. And it
seemed like your writing style."

C.C. stared at Glad. "What?" she asked. "What
are you talking about?"

"Oops," said Glad, banging her forehead with a
fist. "You thought I meant something about you and
Jack Witherspoon. I meant something about your
last paper for me. I might as well tell you. I got an
anonymous note accusing you of plagiarism."

"What?" shrieked C.C. "That's a damn lie! Oh my
God, my God, I can't stand it! I'm pissed off, but totally! I can't stand it."

She collapsed into a chair, put her head down on
the seminar table and wept hysterically.

Glad sat beside her, lit a cigarette, and waited
quietly. Eventually C.C. was able to talk, and did so,
at great length.

Someone was picking on her. She had no idea why.
She hadn't plagiarized her paper for Glad; she had
worked extra hard on it because she loved the class
and knew she wasn't super-smart like all the others.

"Not *all* the others," said Glad gently. "You've
been holding your own pretty well, C.C. You have a
little trouble expressing yourself clearly."

"I know. 'You have trouble handling concepts':
That's what they always say about me. I'm begin-

ning to think that might be another way of saying totally dumb."

Aw.

Glad felt guilty. Poor kid.

She went on to describe her relationship with Mr. Witherspoon.

No, they hadn't used the Oliviero Memorial Practice Room for clandestine assignations. Their relationship was public, but almost pure. Mostly, they sat in the Murray and McCormick Pizzeria and talked for hours about art.

"Oh," said Glad sympathetically. "I didn't know you were interested in art."

"He teaches me," said C.C. simply.

Sometimes they talked about life, too. Sometimes, they took long walks into the woods behind the hockey field. They both totally loved birds. Sometimes they held hands. Sometimes they went to the pool and swam together after hours. Sometimes he just sat in the bleachers and watched her do her Oceanid routines. Sometimes they kissed. Rarely more than that. Pretty rarely.

"And now, poor Mr. Witherspoon!" she said, anguished but no longer crying. "He's in a lot of trouble, all because of me. Do you think they'll fire him, now that President Knight is dead?"

"I don't know," said Glad thoughtfully. "What does he think?"

"I don't know," said C.C., agitated. "That's just it. I haven't seen him at all. He's been avoiding me. I can't stand it. I love him."

She started crying again.

Glad was fresh out of Kleenex. She felt like leaving. She wondered if Chief Chase was waiting in her office. She didn't know what to do.

"Do you know Muffy Work?" she asked.

"Muffy?" asked C.C., stifling a sob. She brought herself under control. "Of course, I know Muffy. She's one of my best friends. We both live in Boroviak Hall; we're both English majors, and we're both Oceanids. She's a good friend of Mr. Witherspoon's, too. In fact, that's how I met him, last year. One day I went into the pizza shop and they were sitting together and asked me to join them. Well, of course, I liked him so much I signed up for Art 101, and you know the rest."

"I guess I do," said Glad. "Do you mind if I leave now, C.C.? I don't want to seem unsympathetic, but I have a lunch date. I'd be glad to talk more this afternoon, though, if . . ."

"Oh, I'll be okay," the girl said, dabbing at her nose with the soggy Kleenex. "I hope you have a nice lunch."

"Thank you. Maybe I'll see you during my office hours tomorrow?"

"Maybe."

Chapter Eleven

March 17: 12:30 p.m.

"Well, did you pick your new leader last night?"

"No. But it's down to two. I have to make a bunch of phone calls tonight, trying to dig up dirty laundry about them. What an *awful* mixed metaphor. . . ." said Glad.

"What's a metaphor?" asked Chief Chase, taking a sip of beer.

They were in Roberto's Diner, enjoying chit-chat and airy persiflage over their cheeseburgers and french-fried onion rings.

"A metaphor is a figure of speech. An implied comparison, like 'he's a real pussycat' or 'she's a—oh, you know, something like 'she's a . . .'"

"Tigress?" suggested Chase.

"I was going to say 'dog,' " said Glad. "But tigress will do. Anyway, you obviously get the idea. So, 'dig up dirt' and 'wash dirty laundry in public' are both metaphorical statements, and it's considered tacky to mix them."

"I see," said Chase, dabbing at a drop of ketchup on his chin with his paper napkin. "That's a good word. Metaphor. Metaphor. I'll remember that. So you have to dig up any dirty laundry these candidate guys have hidden in the closet?"

Glad laughed. "Yeah. But these guys are both women."

"Oh," he said. "Sorry. I'm not usually too bad on that sort of thing. My wife was sort of a libber. I can see it."

"She's given it up?"

"Oh no, that's not what I mean," said Chase, embarrassed. "As far as I know, she's still one. I meant, my wife that *was . . . is* sort of a libber, I guess."

The waitress appeared; they ordered coffee. Glad lit a cigarette.

"Now," said Chase, "what can you tell me that might have some bearing on the murder of Henderson Knight?"

Glad smiled. "You sound just like the inspector in some murder mystery. Who's your favorite author?"

"Oh, Ed McBain, I guess. The Lockridges. I don't know. The Rabbi gives me a royal pain. Oh, excuse me. Have I offended you?"

Glad looked blankly at him. "Why?"

Chase was obviously embarrassed. "I, uh, I guess you might be of the Jewish faith."

Glad laughed warmly. "Oh. Yeah. The Rabbi. Well, yes, I'm half-Jewish, and no, you didn't offend me. For one thing, I'm not religious, and for another, I'm just not easily offended, I guess. Are you Catholic?"

His turn to look surprised. "No," he said. "Congregationalist. Why?"

She banged her forehead penitently. "I'm stupid and see things stereotypically," she said. "I guess I figured all cops were Catholic. And especially in Massachusetts."

"Oh, yeah." He smiled. "But this is southeastern Mass., you know, not Boston. This is degenerate Yankee country. Anyway, let's go back to the murder mysteries."

"Fine. Do you like Agatha Christie?" asked Glad.

"Sure. Of course."

"Dorothy Sayers?"

"Who?"

Glad gleamed with enthusiasm. "Wonderful, oh wonderful!" she cried. "Oh, I just love introducing good people to guaranteed good authors. You must immediately go straight to the Wading River library, and take out everything by Dorothy Sayers. *The Nine Tailors* is the best."

"Okay. I'll do it. May I finish my coffee first?"

"Well, all right."

"And may I interrogate the suspect a bit more?"

"What a thrill! Am I a suspect?"

"Isn't everybody?"

Glad took a thoughtful drag on her cigarette. "Sure," she admitted. "Of course. I'd have to be one, too. But I don't have a key to the pool."

"That's what you say. It's a real mess. I checked with the switchboard lady, and she says nobody— including Knight—borrowed her key on the night of the murder. So someone had to have taken Knight there and let him in before the bashing. I figure there are at least six keys: 1, switchboard; 2, Fowler, the security guard; 3, Silva, the head of security; 4, Christiansen, the gym chairman; 5. Hallett, the swimming instructor; 6. Howard Disher. Disher swears he locked up after the swimming party and his wife corroborates it. Is there a seventh key?"

"I see. That looks bad for Howard Disher, doesn't it?"

"Or for poor old Nick Fowler. The others all have very solid alibis, except maybe Christiansen. After the Oceanid show, she says she drove her babysitter home, then went to bed. Her kids were asleep. She lives in Plymouth, pretty far away."

"She's got a plenty good motive. Did you know good ole Henderson was trying to close down her department?"

"But she's tenured, isn't she?"

"A tenured person can be fired if his or her department or program is eliminated."

"Ah," said Chase. "And what do you think of Mrs. Christiansen?"

Glad took a sip of coffee. It was truly vile. "I hardly know her. I'm not one of the faculty jocks, so she and I seldom have any contact. She's pretty. And a great campus politician. She's saved her department from extinction several times. Do you know that the only course requirement Turnbull still has is two years of phys ed? The students don't have to be able to read or write, but they must have their field hockey and fencing."

Chase smiled. "Do I sense a little professional bitterness?"

"Oh, a little. Charlene Christiansen's an empire-builder, and none of us faculty people like chairmen who build their own departments at the expense of the college. You know, times are tough in academe. If a teacher here loses his or her job, or doesn't get tenure, it doesn't mean another college. It usually means he or she is finished in the profession. If one department is allowed to add an extra person, another loses one. Phys ed has five people; physics, classics, German and Russian are down to two each, and Italian's been eliminated. I didn't like Knight, but I thought he was right to try to cut gym."

Chase sipped his coffee, and made a horrible face. "Okay," he said. "How about other keys?"

"Well," said Glad, "I gather some of the Oceanids have them. That might include C.C. Duxbury, and, through her, possibly Jack Witherspoon. Oh! I just thought of another possibility. I'm not sure about this, but I think Mrs. Pepper—Knight's secretary—might have one. I think she's on vacation now. Anyway, I know she swims a lot, for her back trouble. It's wonderful for disc problems, I hear. So Mary Anne Reilly tells me."

A frown crossed Glad's face.

"Damn. I was planning to call on Mrs. Pepper. I want to ask her about Knight's appointments on his last day alive. But what about Mary Anne Reilly? She's the old lady in astronomy that Knight wouldn't let go to Arizona?"

"Yes. A marvelous person. Lively and smart, tough and youthful."

"Does she have a key to the pool?"

"Oh no," Glad said quickly. "I'm sure she'd have mentioned it. She does swim sometimes for her back trouble, but I think that's always at noon. With Mrs. Pepper and Howard and Barbara Disher."

"Okay," said Chase. "C.C. Duxbury's a possibility, and Witherspoon, through her. Disher or his wife, Mrs. Pepper, Charlene Christiansen, maybe Mary Anne Reilly. Any other whatchamacallums? Oceanographers?"

"Oceanids. Daughters of Oceanus, ancient Greek sea nymphs. Nereids would sound better, but Wellesley already took that name. And Wheaton has Tritons."

"Yeah. Want some more coffee, Professor Gold? Or is it Dr. Gold?"

She smiled. "Oh please, if you don't feel up to Ms. you could call me Miss Gold. Or if you're willing to be called Bob or Jerry or whatever instead of Chief, you could call me Glad."

Pretty dimple. Small boobs, but that was okay with Chase. Evelyn, his ex-wife, had the flip-em-over-your-shoulder variety. Really a bit much.

"My name is Alden. You could call me Al, but I really am uncommonly fond of 'Chief.' "

Wonderful smile, absolutely Leslie Howard. Or, as Mandy Tweedy had suggested, Dick Cavett. Nice voice. Not lacking in humor.

"I must admit," she said, "that I have a shameful secret fondness for 'Doctor,' too, but since we've shared french fries together, I think I should call you Al. Unless it would be improper, in a suspect."

"Okay, Glad."

Chief Chase smiled; Professor Gold smiled. Their

eyes met full on; both stopped smiling abruptly. One of those sudden shivers of frank sexual recognition. Glad looked down at her coffee, embarrassed, warm.

Chase cleared his throat. "Do you have lots of boyfriends?" he asked.

She giggled. "Oh, at least one per MLA meeting."

He looked blank.

"The Modern Language Association. Professors' convention, once a year. Scholarly papers, job hunting slave market, panel discussions on recent trends in structural analysis of film. But it usually turns out that the guy teaches in Vancouver or Hawaii, or hates Tennyson, or has a wife and eight kids at home or something. How about you? Lots of girl friends?"

"Some. Nothing to write home about. By the way, I've never read Tennyson."

"Yes you have. Everybody reads 'Crossing the Bar' in high school."

Chase frowned. " 'And as he crossed the second bar, he murmured, "well, all right so far." ' Some guy falling out of a window."

"No, you're not trying. 'Sunset and evening star, and one clear call for me.' Ring any bells?"

"Sure. I remember that. So, you don't like guys who don't like Tennyson. Hmm." He frowned with fake anxiety.

A look of teacherly enthusiasm lit up Glad's rather severe face. "Aha!" she said, "a challenge! You know, only the very sappiest Tennyson gets into anthologies. There are absolute reams of simply exquisite, wonderful, passionate, thoughtful, smashing stuff by Tennyson that nobody ever reads or even knows about. I can make you like Tennyson. I can make you love Tennyson."

"My place or yours?" He smiled.

She glanced involuntarily at her watch.

"I saw that," he pounced triumphantly.

"Oops," she said. "Okay. I have a seminar at three-thirty."

"It's only one-fifteen. I'm serious. I'd like you to teach me to love Tennyson. I dare you. I'm a real challenge. Semi-literate pig, you know."

"You put some of that on, don't you?" she asked.

"A little," he admitted. "My place or yours?"

"Well," she said dubiously, "I doubt you have 'Tithonus' or 'Maud' at your house."

"Mabel might still be there, but I'm almost sure Tithonus has left."

She held her nose. "Unworthy, oh, unworthy," she said. "I live quite close to here, on Main Street."

"I know."

"You know?"

"I'm the head fuzz, remember? It's a small town. I know where almost everybody lives. You had a break two years ago, black-and-white TV, good stereo, camera, typewriter, binoculars and some costume jewelry."

"You're amazing," she said with respect. "But you're wrong about the binoculars."

"Oh well. I admit I was guessing about the stuff. That's what they usually take from professors."

"Oh really? What do they take from other Wading River people?"

"Pretty much the same, but the TVs are color, and there's usually a gun or two, and no typewriter."

"Fascinating."

He knew things she didn't know. He had his own life, his own job, his own personality. He was not a professor. She trembled slightly. She lit a cigarette.

Chase looked at her. This girl was exciting. But she wasn't a girl. Her long, slim, plaid legs reached over to his side of the table. He wanted to lean down and touch them. Her blue-gray sweater was fuzzy, and looked very soft. He wanted to reach across the table and touch her smooth, intelligent face. Her smooth straight hair. She looked up at him, and stubbed her cigarette out without looking away from his eyes. This time, he looked away first, embarrassed at the urgency of his lust.

"Don't you have to go back to work?" she asked in a soft voice.

"I'm the boss," he said boastfully. "I'll radio the station and tell them I'm following up something hot."

She made an awful face, but didn't seem really offended.

She insisted on paying for herself. "You can't buy me with onion rings," she said.

They went to his car.

She was amused by his radio. Pleased, like a little kid. "Do you have a siren?" she asked enthusiastically.

"And a flashing blue light."

"Do you carry a gun?"

"Not anymore. I carry the weight of my authority."

"Good," she said firmly.

She seemed relieved. So was he. Some women were awfully turned on by a gun. Chase didn't quite like that.

Her house was small, nicely furnished, pleasantly messy with books and papers. Tiny little bedroom. Old-fashioned shiny brass bedframe, pretty flowered quilt.

She was a medley of good smells—something lemony on her straight smooth hair, a mixture of smoke and sweet flowers on her fuzzy blue sweater, something like almonds on her long slim nervous fingers; she trembled all over. Her skin was very white, her triangle very dark and soft, her body not so lean as it looked in clothes but warm and yielding and jumpily responsive to every touch. He touched and murmured and inhaled her sweet bouquet of food and smoke and flowers, and she touched him with her long almond fingers, unbuttoned, unbuckled, unzipped him, released him, held him then imprisoned, caught and kept him. Kept him and, finally, set him astonishingly free.

"I'm sorry," he said. "Too quick. Overeager."

"It was good," she said. "You make me happy."

"Really?"

"Really."

"Well, we'll have to practice till we get it right."

"Okay. Good idea."

"Oh, Glad."

She giggled. "That's Dr. Gold, please."

He bit her shoulder lightly.

"Oh, Chief," she murmured.

He slapped her round little fanny. "Anyone for Tennyson?" he asked jovially.

"Oh please," she groaned. "Everyone makes that joke and expects me to laugh. It's like having a funny name."

"Sorry." He sounded hurt.

"Oh, Alden, I'm sorry you're sorry." She kissed him.

He kissed her.

"Want a drink?" She sat up.

"Heavens, ma'am," he said, "not while I'm on duty. But I'll tell you what I would like."

"Name it."

"Read me a poem."

"Really?"

"Sure. Tennyson."

So they sat in bed, and she read him "The Kraken" and "Mariana," and he liked them, or said he did. They kissed and agreed to meet for a drink after her dirt-digging phone calls that evening.

"And I think," she said, "that I'd better tell you about Muffy Work and C.C. Duxbury because there's something going on there, I think, that may be relevant to the murder."

"Great," said Chase. "Call me when you're through with your work tonight. But don't you think you'd better get dressed now?"

Glad looked at her bedside clock and leaped to her feet like a demon. "Oh, damn, *damn,*" she wailed, anguished. "My seminar! Oh damn, oh hell."

She flew around the room, assembling her clothes, combing hair, buttoning, zipping, buckling, wailing, "I'm so bad! I'm a bad person!"

"Not so very bad," said Chase, tying his shoes calmly. "If you were, I'd arrest you."

She laughed and kissed him on his limp fair hair. "Okay," she said. "I'm the teacher, after all. They can't start till I get there."

Chapter Twelve

March 17: 6:30 p.m.

GLAD WAS thoroughly frustrated. It sounded so easy: just call Berkeley and New York and find out about the candidates' graduate careers. First, she called Professor Oddo, Diane Day's thesis adviser, in New York. The line was busy twice; then there was no answer. At Berkeley, nobody seemed to know that Lucille Walker England had ever existed, even though Glad, having the vita right in front of her, was able to supply precise dates, names of courses, titles of M.A. and Ph.D. dissertations and so forth. The assistant registrar was blank, and distinctly uninterested in this long distance call about one of her alums who might become the first woman president of Turnbull College.

"I'm afraid I can't help you, madam," she said curtly. "This is a very busy time for us."

Glad dragged viciously on her cigarette, and spoke in a controlled voice: "Then may I speak to the registrar, please? There must be some record for Lucille Walker. She received her degree in 1960."

"Well, I'm very sorry, madam, but that was a long time ago, and the records would be extremely hard to locate. I told you, this is a busy time for us; we are computing grade point averages."

Glad smashed her cigarette into the ashtray. "May I please speak to the registrar?"

"This is the registrar's office. The registrar is not available."

"Is there a graduate alumni secretary or an alumni records office?"

"Yes, of course there is."

"Would you have your operator switch me to that extension, please?"

"All right, madam."

Glad was, of course, cut off.

She said a loud word into the buzzing receiver, paced around the kitchen for a minute, got herself a beer and went back to the telephone. Still no answer at Professor Oddo's.

The Berkeley alumni records office was little better. The assistant there was very sweet, even inclined to chat, but she had only been at this job, she explained, for two weeks, and had no idea where 1960 was kept. Perhaps Mrs. Golden would like to speak to the history department? The secretary there was a rill darling, and rill old. She might even remember this Lucille Ryder.

Glad was switched to the history secretary who did, vaguely, remember someone named Lucille, from about '60. No, she had no records of graduate student grades; they would be in the alumni records office. No, she had no idea which professors might have had Lucille Walker as a student. Professor Dill, the thesis adviser, was long dead. Of course, there was Professor Hinnerschütz. He was certainly old enough to have taught this girl, and he was himself a distinguished scholar. Yes, as a matter of fact, he was in his office right now. She would have Glad switched to his extension.

At last.

"Hello?"

"Professor Hinnerschütz? This is Glad Gold. I'm an English professor at Turnbull College in Massachusetts."

"Do I know you, my dear?" asked a courtly, gentle, aged voice.

Glad was warm with relief and gratitude.

"No, sir," she said. "I am calling you because I am on a presidential search committee for Turnbull College, and a former student of yours, Lucille Walker England, is one of our top candidates. I've been delegated to find out what I can about Lucille Walker's career as a graduate student. Do you remember her, by any chance?"

"Perfectly, my dear."

Not only gratitude. Glad felt real affection for dear Professor Hinnerschütz.

"Could you tell me something about her?"

"Beautiful girl, if you admire strong noses. Lucille Walker . . . had a terrible time with German. German. Goethe, Schiller, Mann, Bonn, Swann, Proust . . ."

"Pardon me? Professor Hinnerschütz?"

"Do I know you, my dear?"

"You were telling me about Lucille Walker. She was in American history, got her degree in '60. You said she had a problem with German. She was—is—tall, with dark hair and a rather prominent nose? Her dissertation was called 'The Age of Chester A. Arthur.' "

"Oh yes, my dear, of course. I remember. You see, I was afraid I was supposed to know you, and had forgotten and offended you. I've been doing that lately. Forgot my own nephew yesterday. Couldn't remember his name to save my soul."

He didn't seem inclined to continue.

"Oh. Well, I'm sorry, sir. I'm really sorry to have taken your time like this. . . ."

"Don't mention it!" said the old professor graciously. "My pleasure, my dear. Lucille Walker. German. As a matter of fact, I seem to recall that there's someone who could tell you more about Lucille Walker than I can. . . ."

"Oh? That would be very good to know, sir."

"Oh, yes," he chuckled. "Fellow who used to teach here, rather smitten with Lucille, we all thought."

"Could you possibly tell me his name?" Glad poised her pencil, ready.

"Ah yes. Not a very nice fellow, perhaps, but smart. Good-looking. Good clothes. Ended up somewhere in your neck of the woods, I believe. . . ."

"And his name is—?"

"Knight. Henderson Neville Knight."

Pause. Glad put her pencil down. "Thank you, Professor Hinnerschütz. You've been very good to spare me some of your time."

"No trouble, my dear. It's been a real pleasure talking to you. But I must say, I do think you're wasting your time, a bit."

"Oh? Why do you say so?"

"Berkeley already has a president. I don't believe we need a new one at the moment."

Glad said goodbye, most politely. She hoped the other search committee members were having better luck.

Well, Day was younger; her thesis adviser was still alive, even if he didn't answer his phone, and her graduate records were all included in a full, up-to-date dossier, so there wouldn't be a necessity to go through one of those registrar's office runarounds for her.

Glad dialed Professor Oddo again. This time, after a number of rings, the phone was picked up. A little kid's voice. "Heyyo?"

"Hello? May I speak to Professor Oddo, please?"

"My daddy isn't here. Who are you?"

"I'm a, I'm a professor, like your daddy."

"But you're a yady."

Glad lit a cigarette. "Well, honey, ladies can be professors, too."

"My mommy isn't a professor. She's a head shrinker."

Glad laughed. "Okay, that's fine too. May I speak to your mommy?"

"No. My mommy is in Paris with my daddy. They yeft us home with the yousy babysitter."

Glad exhaled wearily. "Okay. May I speak to the babysitter, please?"

"Sure you can. But she doesn't talk in Engyish."

"What language does she talk in, honey?"

"Yatvian."

"Oh boy. Well. Okay . . . I guess I'll say goodbye now. It's been fun talking to you."

"All right. 'Bye."

Damn damn damn. Glad felt utterly defeated. She sifted through the great sheaf of papers she had on Day and England, looking for names, addresses, phone numbers. Nothing relevant. Glad had a friend at Columbia, in English, but he was too young to have known Diane Day. Damn. It was all ridiculous.

Oh well, give up. Time to take a bath, get beautiful for the Chief. Call him first? No. Bath first. Think about what to tell him. C.C. and Muffy . . .

She stuffed all the highly secret papers about Day and England into her briefcase. Better keep them in the office . . . More chance of mixing them up with her own clutter at home.

The phone rang. It was Bill Schuster, the trustee.

"Oh, Mr. Schuster, I've been having a terrible time trying to find out about our candidates. Just an awful runaround. Day's thesis adviser is in Europe, and nobody at Berkeley seems to remember anything about England, except one senile guy who remembers she had a big nose and trouble with German."

Bill was kind. "Then why don't you quit?" he advised. "I've already called several people at Osborne, and they're all very happy with Mrs. Day. And Jane Della Rosa spoke to a couple of administrators and a trustee at Stott, and they're equally enthusiastic about Mrs. England. Miss Reilly tells me that Mrs.

England's book on Chester Arthur received favorable reviews, and that Mrs. Day's poetry is highly regarded by people who like that sort of thing. It's beginning to look as though we can't go wrong with either one."

"What good news!"

"So I've arranged for each of them to come here for dinner and to give us a brief formal talk about the future of Turnbull. Mrs. England has graciously agreed to come tomorrow night, and we'll have Mrs. Day the following night. Seven o'clock in the president's dining room at the college. All right with you? Can you make it to both dinners?"

"Fine. I do feel bad about not coming up with anything."

"Don't. We've all worked hard, and we're on the homestretch now. See you tomorrow?"

"Yes. Absolutely. Thanks for calling, Mr. Schuster. Goodbye."

She soaked a long time in the tub, uneasy, thinking about C.C. Duxbury, about the swimming pool, about Henderson Neville Knight. Knight the Upright. Fallen low. The man of principle. The principal. The prince. The Machiavelli of Turnbull who ruined adulterers' lives, but manipulated the faculty to promote himself.

Not Howard Disher. He'd have done it earlier when he was fired. He did have a key to the pool. But Howard was a dear teddy bear. Family man. Sweet man.

Not C.C. surely. Nor Jack Witherspoon. Both too innocent. Too young, too romantic. Too soft.

Please, God, not Mary Anne.

Charlene Christiansen was a mother. Little kids. Would a mother of little kids commit murder just to save her department?

Something, something must have happened the day Knight was killed. Someone was pushed too hard.

The phone rang. Glad forced herself out of the warm lovely tub, down to the kitchen, freezing in a threadbare towel, dripping on the linoleum.

It was the Chief; his voice was full of controlled excitement. "Hi, Doctor, I think I'm on to something. You finished with your phoning?"

"Yes. It was a washout. You want to call off our drink?"

"Nope. But I want to pick you up soon and take a short walk around the campus with you before we have our drink. Can you be ready in five minutes?"

"I'll try. I'm only wearing a towel right now. The front door will be unlocked. Just come on in, and I'll be down as fast as I can."

"Don't do that," he said seriously.

"Don't dress? Don't be down as fast as I can?"

"Don't leave the door unlocked."

"Oh. What will you do, bust it down?"

"Don't smart-mouth me, Doctor."

"Okay, Chief. Whatever you say."

Strange. Actually she was all dressed by the time he rang her bell. Red cords, good perfume, eyeliner, the whole bit.

He was not in uniform. He looked terrific, slim, graceful, full of energy and very young, in an Irish sweater and dark green cords.

They strolled over to the campus. It was breezy, but not too cold, and walking was rather pleasant.

At Chase's request they started at the president's house. They stood in front of the gracious large colonial for a few minutes, looking down Main Street.

"Can you see the natatorium from here?" asked the Chief.

"No," said Glad. "Boroviak Hall is in the way."

"Do you suppose Knight could see it from his side windows?"

"There would be a direct view through the garden. I suppose he could see lights, at least. But there's a lot of shrubbery beside the house."

"Let's walk along Main, then turn onto Forsythe and end up at the pool. You tell me the names of the buildings and houses on the way."

They walked slowly.

"That's Boroviak Hall," said Glad, pointing to a small, ivy-covered brick dormitory next to the president's side garden. "C.C. Duxbury lives there. And that's Walgreen, another dorm. That little cottage next to the pool is the alumnae guest house. The gray house across Forsythe Street is Howard Disher's."

They turned the corner and stood in front of the Pearce pool building, looking back at the president's house.

"Yes. Look," said Glad. "You can see lights in his house from here. Melanie's there. Poor lady. She's going to miss those roses."

"So Knight walked through his garden to that side gate there," said Chase softly. "It was after midnight. His wife was asleep. Nobody saw him walking over here."

"Except . . . one person," said Glad.

"Yes. Maybe that person walked with him? Followed him? Or was that person waiting at the pool already?"

Glad was shivering a little. It was breezy. "Someone could have been waiting for Prexy, hiding in the shrubbery in his garden," she suggested. "He sees lights in the pool, walks through his garden to investigate—maybe we left a light on when we were swimming? And someone follows him into the building and bashes him on the head."

"Okay," said Chase. "But how does Knight get into the pool building? And does it really make sense for the president of a college to investigate lights or funny noises by himself? Wouldn't he just pick up the phone and call a security guard?"

"I guess he would," admitted Glad. "He must

have had a reason for leaving his house after midnight."

"A girl friend?" asked Chase.

"Prexy?" exclaimed Glad, shocked. "Not him. Never. He was utterly, absolutely moralistic about sexual things. I'd sooner believe him capable of murder. Do we have to go inside?"

"No. Let's go get our drink."

"Fine," she said. "And I'll tell you about C.C. and Muffy before I forget, and you can tell me what *you're* on to."

"Oh, it's probably nothing," he said casually. "Routine police work, only. Methodical, unimaginative, you know. Not the sort of thing your Lord Peter Wimsey would dirty himself with."

Glad grabbed Chase's arm impulsively. "You've started Dorothy Sayers already," she said happily. "How did you have time this afternoon, along with your routine and all?"

"The Chief doesn't actually *do* the routine police work, you understand," he said, smiling. "He orders it done. I read the papers in Mrs. Pepper's desk. Very interesting. Then I went to the library, and while I was eating a lonely cheeseburger at Roberto's, I started reading *Gaudy Night.*"

"You ate another cheeseburger at Roberto's, after today's lunch there? Our place?"

"It wasn't the same," he admitted. "Bit too rare, in fact. And *Gaudy Night* is not exactly what I'd call fast-paced or action-packed. And when do I get to the obligatory sex scene? I'm already on page one-twenty."

"Oh dear. Did you ever start with the wrong one!"

"Just kidding. Don't worry. I kind of like her way of writing."

"Oh, good!" Glad beamed.

They had arrived at Herb and Ina's Place, a moderately seedy bar. They found a dark booth and ordered beer.

"One sentence in that book," continued Chase, "I

found really funny. Where this teddibly British professor lady is worried about her sanity, and says 'I'm
afraid I shall go potty.' Now, as a father of two children who have gone through toilet training, I call
that a funny line."

Glad laughed and sipped her beer, and caught his
eye, and all the thrill returned.

Chase looked down into his beer. "Tell me about
Muffy and C.C. Do all your students have names
like that?"

"One year I had an advanced class with only two
students, C.C. and Didi. I kept expecting two more to
join us: A.A. and B.B."

She told him everything she remembered about
the anonymous notes and her amateur detective
work. He was much interested, but not inclined to
see any obvious connection between the notes and
the murder of President Knight.

After an hour or so, he walked her home. On the
way, he looked at every single car parked on Main
Street.

"What are you doing?" she asked finally.

"Force of habit," he laughed. "Patrolmen in small
towns spend a lot of time looking at and for strange
cars. There, for example, is a rented car, from Rhode
Island."

"It's a free country, isn't it, Chief?" asked Glad.

"Where'd you get that idea?" he countered; then
he stopped her and kissed her warmly.

Her house was a mess.

Books, papers, all over the floor, drawers emptied,
her jewelry gone. The stereo, TV and typewriter
were all miraculously still there.

"He must have heard someone coming," said
Chase calmly. "You were lucky, Doctor. Oh, look.
That's how he got in."

The pane of glass on the kitchen door had been
smashed with a rock; a hand had reached in through
the broken glass to unlock it.

Glad was sitting at the kitchen table, staring dumbly at the rubble around her.

The Chief put his arm around her. "For your protection, ma'am," he said, "I think I had better spend the night here. It's obligatory."

Chapter Thirteen

March 18: 6:50 p.m.

THE SEARCH COMMITTEE ladies were conferring again. Primping, powdering, combing and caucusing in the ladies' lounge.

"I still don't trust Palmer Jordan not to pull a fast one," said Jane Della Rosa, as she applied a fresh coat of bright pink lipstick. She kissed a paper towel to blot her mouth, and continued. "He seems to accept that it's going to be either Day or England, but I'm suspicious of his volunteering to drive to Providence this afternoon to meet England at the airport. What'll you bet that all the way to Wading River he's been telling her what crappy financial shape Turnbull's in?"

"That's a sobering thought," said Mary Anne. "He's also scheduled to drive Diane Day down from Boston tomorrow night."

"Omigod," gasped Olympia, who was brushing her wonderful dark hair. "Do you mean he might be talking them into dropping out of the search?"

"That seems to be the idea," said Glad, anxiously brushing some cigarette ashes off her velvet blazer. "Then, if both of them drop out, he can re-introduce Mr. Williams, as the only finalist courageous enough to face our fiscal problems."

Mary Anne tucked in a few stray hairs and suggested, "Maybe one of us should volunteer to drive them back to the airport, and warn them about Palmer's forked tongue. I'd do it myself, but this is a perfect night for observing, and I was planning to use the telescope after dinner. . . ."

"I'll do it," said Olympia eagerly.

Glad, thinking that Olympia's driving would surely eliminate at least one of the candidates if Palmer Jordan's talking didn't, concluded, "No, Olympia, that's unnecessary. You've done all the driving. I'll be happy to do it."

"No use," put in the newspaperwoman. "Lucille England's staying in the alum guest house tonight; Bill Schuster's driving her to the airport tomorrow morning, while you girls are in school. And Diane Day is going to be picked up after the dinner tomorrow night by a friend who lives in Cambridge."

"Ah well," said Olympia, "then we'll just have to be persuasive at dinner about the charm of Turnbull and the challenge and all that. And just hope our paranoid fantasies about Palmer are wrong."

At that moment Muffy Work bounced into the ladies' room, leading Annette Gosling, a quiet, smart black senior who was the other student member of the search committee.

"Oh hi, everybody!" bubbled Muffy. "Aren't you all just excited to death? I can hardly wait for this dinner!" She stepped into a stall.

"Mrs. England just arrived, with Mr. Jordan," said Annette, smiling shyly.

"Oops," said Glad, taking one more look in the mirror at her limp hair and her definitely puffy-looking eyes. "We'd better go out."

"You look tired," said Mary Anne sympathetically.

"I was up late," said Glad. Alden had asked her not to mention the burglary to anyone. It was most mysterious: the jewelry, which had been the only stuff taken, had been found by Chase in the morning, in a little heap, half-buried under a bush beside the back door. Some crazy kind of vandalism. Apparently.

Muffy Work bounced out of the john into the mirrored lounge where the women were talking; at the same moment, Lucille Walker England entered the lounge from the outside lobby.

The women all turned to greet her, but Muffy got there first, and shook the candidate's hand vigorously. "It's so great to see you again, Mrs. England," she gushed. "I just love your suit!"

Lucille England was wearing a handsome, tweedy suit—the same one she had worn to the initial interview. Her gray hair was beautifully cut, and her hawk nose and large bright eyes gave her face a strong, vivid appeal. She had a fine tall figure, too: Glad enjoyed looking straight across into the intelligent blue eyes. All in all, she had the sort of presence that inspires confidence. In fact, Glad found herself trying desperately to remember Diane Day, and just why she had been so impressed by her.

"I'm delighted to see you again, Muffy, and Annette," said Mrs. England, in her rich alto voice. Mary Anne glowed with obvious pride in her candidate's presidential manner.

"And Professor Principe—so glad you could be here. Professor Gold—do I have that right? From English? Miss Della Rosa, of course, all the way from New York? This search must be exhausting you all. What with meeting all the candidates and reading, I'm sure, reams of recommendations and checking everyone's background, and now, these dinners. Professor Reilly, how are your observations of double stars coming along?"

Mary Anne smiled modestly. "I was just telling the others I plan to put in a night at the observatory after our dinner," she said. "It's the clearest night we've had in weeks."

"Well, I hope you find what you're looking for," said Lucille England affectionately, grasping both of

Mary Anne's hands in her own for a moment. "Real science—real scholarship—is a lonely process." Then she saw that she was embarrassing Mary Anne, and dropped the hands instantly. "I have the profoundest respect for you, Miss Reilly."

"Don't you consider yourself a scholar, Mrs. England?" asked Glad.

The candidate laughed heartily, a low, likable laugh. "Indeed, I don't," she said earnestly. "I wrote a book once. But now, I am only an administrator—I see my function as really a rather humble one, laboring to make your work possible. The teachers and scholars—they are the college. We administrators just oversee the housekeeping details, so that you and, of course, the students, can get on with the real business of learning."

"How poetic," said Olympia.

Mrs. England laughed again, self-deprecatingly. "Well, maybe it was a little oratorical for a ladies' room speech," she admitted. "I was cribbing from the spontaneous remarks I'm planning to make at dinner tonight."

Glad laughed, relieved to find humor as well as stage presence in Mrs. England.

"Shall we join the gentlemen?" asked the candidate.

"Oh yes," said Muffy. "I just love the trustees."

Jane Della Rosa winced.

They joined the gentlemen, who were talking about a prestigious law school at which a white male caucus had just been formed.

The Turnbull president's dining room was not so elegant as most of the Boston dining rooms in which the committee usually met, and the waitress was a student, but the dinner was almost as good as they were accustomed to: steak with mushrooms, potatoes au gratin, broccoli, creme de menthe parfait. And acceptable wine. The college food service, Institution Food Inc. (IFI for short), was apparently trying to im-press the potential new president in order to retain its lucrative contract with the college.

"It's not all beige," said Glad, wonderingly, to Olympia.

Conversation was lively and general. Even Palmer Jordan was jovial, and told several fairly funny stories.

Lucille England was in top form. She talked sensibly about finances, about co-education, which she thought Turnbull would be unwise to adopt; about the liberal arts, which she considered to be still the best practical education for the highest professions; and about the faculty's role in college governance.

"Whatever happened to the word 'government?'" whispered Glad to Olympia.

"I know, I know," whispered Olympia. "She does use academic jargon a bit. But you can't fault her on content, can you?"

"She's smooth," murmured Glad. "Hell, I admit it; she's good. But don't make your mind up till we've seen Day again."

"Okay. But shut up now; Jordan's looking at us."

At the same time, Jane Della Rosa was holding a cigarette in her left hand, and writing a note to Mary Anne Reilly with her right, in her lap.

"I must have been wrong about Jordan," said the note. "This lady's running."

Mary Anne read the note surreptitiously and nodded slowly without looking at Jane. Then she fished a pen out of her pocketbook and added to the note, "Maybe he tried and failed."

Jane sipped her coffee slowly, then glanced at the note, and nodded once, barely removing her smiling gaze away from Lucille England.

The dinner concluded with a brief formal talk. The candidate didn't use notes, was utterly cool and spoke beautifully: her rich, low voice was just loud enough, just slow enough, just right. She did, however, say "presently" for "at present," and, once, "different than." To be fair, it was a complicated sentence, and many words intervened between the "different" and the "than," but still . . . Glad found herself thinking that Henderson Neville Knight would *never* have said "different than." He was a self-righteous bastard and a hypocrite—but his English was beyond reproach.

Does the chief say "different than"?

Is it proper to sleep with a man before you even know whether or not he says "different than?"

Well. It was a good speech, not only well spoken, but well written, if a bit predictable. About the role of the women's college in the America of today. Challenge, exciting time to live in as a woman, responsibility for leadership, all that.

Glad secretly unbuttoned her waistband. Thank God for overblouses.

The speech was over. Lucille England was thanking them all, and doing a gracious little bit about how she wouldn't be sore if they decided that someone else would be more right for the Turnbull community.

Mary Anne rose and announced that she was off to observe double stars. Olympia, too, said she was planning to do some work in her office. The others all exchanged goodbyes.

As the search committee was filing out of the dining room and into the coat room, Muffy said, "Ooh, that's so brave of you, Miss Reilly! Aren't you scared, going over to the observatory all alone, at night?"

"No," said Mary Anne, picking up her old leather briefcase.

"Can I help you with that, Miss Reilly?" asked Lucille England. "It looks heavy."

"Heavens, no," laughed Mary Anne.

"Allow me," said Palmer Jordan, and wrestled her for it.

"Please," said Mary Anne, "it's good of you to of-

fer, but I'm quite capable of carrying my own briefcase. Been doing it for thirty years."

Annette Gosling was talking to Muffy. "Come off
it, Muffy," she said. "You're not scared of the dark
either. You go over to the pool at night all the time to
practice your Oceanid stuff, don't you?"

Muffy was struggling into her sweater; she didn't
reply.

Glad, who was putting on her coat, touched Muffy's
sleeve. "That right?" she asked, in a friendly voice.
"Do you swim at night, alone? I think that's marvelous. Do you?"

"Not very often," said Muffy quietly, opening the
front door.

"Do you have a key to the pool?" asked Glad, following Muffy, who was walking rather quickly on
the path that led toward Forsythe Street.

"Sure she does," called Annette, as she started
in the opposite direction. At that precise moment,
Muffy was shaking her head and saying no.

"I want to talk to you, Muffy," said Glad, hurrying
after the bouncing student.

Chapter Fourteen

March 18: 9:05 p.m.

PALMER JORDAN was the last one left in the building. After losing the battle for Mary Anne's briefcase, the portly trustee discovered that he needed to use the men's room, so he said goodbye to the last committee members and went back through the lounge, past the president's dining room.

As he was washing his hands, he heard a noise out in the lounge.

What's that? he thought jumpily. Footsteps. Definitely footsteps. He thought of going back into a cubicle and locking himself in; then he caught a glimpse of himself in the mirror. What a fine big man he was, to be sure. Indeed, a corporation president! In fact, chairman of the board of Turnbull! People are afraid of me, he thought proudly, and stood his ground in front of the washbowl.

In the mirror he saw the door to the men's room opening slowly.

"Excuse me?" asked a polite, young voice. "Is the search committee all over?"

It was a little fair-haired guy—looked as if you could knock him over with a feather. Must be some student's boyfriend. A townie.

"What are you doing here, young man?" thundered Palmer Jordan, conscious of his impressive size and commanding manner. "If you're not out of here in one minute, I'll turn you over to a security guard!"

The little guy actually had the nerve to smile. "I was looking for Professor Gold," he said softly, "but I guess she's left already." He turned to go, but Jordan grabbed him by his corduroy sleeve.

"Do you have some identification?" he demanded curtly.

The young man, infuriatingly, smiled again. "You're gonna love this," he said, and fished a plastic card and a small piece of metal out of his pocket.

"Hmph. Well. Chief Chase, hum. Sorry. Should wear a uniform. Anyway, nobody here but me; I was just leaving."

"May I ask you for some identification, sir?" said Chase solemnly.

Palmer Jordan took a while finding his driver's license. Finally, he handed it over, mute.

"Thank you very much, Mr. Jordan," said Chase, glancing and handing it back. "Can you tell me how long ago Professor Gold left?"

"Maybe ten minutes ago. Probably going home."

Chase frowned. "I was just at her house; she isn't there. Her car is still there. I really need to find her: police business."

" 'Fraid I can't help you, Chief."

"Well, thanks anyway."

"Hmph. Okay. 'Night."

Both men left the building. Jordan went to his big car, which was parked nearby, on Burton Street. Chase headed across the campus, toward Dahl.

When he arrived at the building, however, he saw that she wasn't there; no lights were on in the office windows. He tried the door; it was locked. He felt mildly anxious, and his anxiety was increased considerably when a voice behind him said, "Stop right there, fella!"

It was a security guard. A new guy. Must be Nick Fowler's replacement. Again, Chase went through the business of showing his identification. With rather less pleasure this time.

The guard didn't know who Glad was, but he knew there were women faculty members working in Worthley Hall, and in Marshall; he had seen their lights.

"No," said Chase. "Her office is in Dahl. Her car is parked on Main Street, so she must be somewhere near here."

"What's she look like?" asked the guard, eager to please.

"Tall. Straight dark hair. Brown coat."

"Good-looking?"

Chase paused. "Yes. Probably smoking a cigarette."

"Oh, yeah. I think I seen her. Walking with a student, cute little blonde. Bubbly type. Talking a lot. Over toward the dorm on Forsythe Street. You say the lady's good-looking?"

"Very."

"Matter of opinion."

"Okay, thanks." Hurrying, Chase retraced his steps across the campus.

Glad was bullying Muffy. Using her authority as a professor, and relying on Muffy's obsequiousness, she had persuaded Muffy to accompany her to the pool, and to unlock the door. Yes, Muffy admitted, she had a key.

Lots of Oceanids did, but, said Muffy, she didn't want it to get around, because it was sort of illegal, you know.

"I have a *great* idea!" said Glad. "Let's have a quick swim before we go home!"

Muffy looked frankly astonished. Professor Gold was no athlete, and she always kept a certain distance between herself and students. "I don't know," Muffy said, hesitating. "I've got a paper to write. . . ."

"Oh, I think it would be such fun. Please, Muffy? Just a quick lap or two?"

Muffy agreed reluctantly. She hardly bounced at all.

They entered the pool building; Glad's glasses steamed up instantly. She had a flash of anxiety remembering the last time she had entered this building, and her grisly discovery then.

They went into the dressing room. Muffy, as an Oceanid, had her own locker and an assortment of sexy bathing costumes. Glad had to settle for one of the holy black cotton tank suits.

The natatorium was kept very warm, and Glad, as she stripped, felt sweaty and cold at the same time.

Muffy, naked, had a darling, taut little body.

Glad laughed ruefully. "This place is a great equalizer. You know, Muffy, we professors feel pretty big and superior out there in the classrooms and on campus. In here, you students with your lovely young bodies have it all over us!"

Muffy said quietly, "I know." She threw her tiny green underpants on a bench and slipped neatly into her purple nylon Oceanid suit. Glad pulled the shapeless cotton tank suit up over her not-very-firm stomach and not-very-big breasts.

"Well," said Muffy, "you wanted to swim, Professor Gold. So let's swim."

They entered the pool room. Muffy flipped on the underwater lights, then dove in. She swam a length in almost total silence; it was amazing how rapidly she could swim without splashing or puffing or chugging. Her Oceanid training, no doubt: the water seemed to offer her no resistance at all. Glad stood at the shallow end, gazing nearsightedly at the perfectly clear water, staring at the place where a corpse had floated, undulating, only a few days before. The baseball equipment was gone.

"Come on in; it's super," bubbled Muffy.

Glad couldn't speak. She just stood and stared at the clean blue water.

Muffy stood up in the water, not far from where Knight's body had been. She gave Glad a crooked smile.

"Why are we here?" the student asked suddenly.

Glad sat down on the edge and let her long legs dangle in the lovely water. She looked straight at Muffy; Muffy averted her gaze.

"I want to know the truth," said Glad, as firmly as she could manage. Her heart pounded as Muffy waded closer to her.

"The truth about what?" asked Muffy, innocently.

"Do you write anonymous notes with a brown felt-tip pen?"

Muffy waded even closer, and stood very near Glad's long, trembling legs. The student looked directly into Glad's eyes, and said, "Yes." She wasn't bubbling at all.

"Are you in love with Jack Witherspoon?" asked Glad, trying not to flinch as Muffy took a step even closer.

Muffy put her tiny hands on Glad's knees; Glad recoiled instinctively; Muffy grasped her wrists and pulled with an athlete's strength; Glad slid, tumbling gracelessly into the water.

"Come on, Professor Gold, you were the one who wanted to swim."

Glad was afraid. Once, as a child, she had almost drowned, and ever since she had been rather insecure in the water; Muffy was a pro. Muffy was pulling her, gently but firmly, into the deeper water.

Glad tried to stand firm, but found herself helpless to resist the relentless tugging.

"Come on, swim!" insisted Muffy.

Glad broke away, and stupidly started to swim, chugging noisily, panting, toward the deep end. She swam as fast as she could; Muffy stayed right behind her all the way, apparently without effort.

When they were almost at the end of the pool, Glad put out a hand and grabbed the edge. Muffy, too, held out her hand—toward Glad. "Don't touch me," screamed Glad, panicking. Muffy withdrew her hand.

She laughed a bubbly little laugh and stayed very near Glad, treading water easily. "Don't panic, Professor Gold," she said in a casual voice. "I could have, you know, drowned you before now, if I'd wanted to. You know what I mean?"

"I know," said Glad.

"I do love Jack Witherspoon."

Glad nodded. "And hate him, too."

"Of course," admitted Muffy unemotionally. "He's an immoral person. Like, he balls his students."

"Didn't he—uh—ball you, before C.C.?"

"No," said Muffy nastily. "He never did. I wouldn't let him, you know. So he, like, turned to her."

"And you told President Knight."

"Yes."

"Did you bring Knight here?"

Muffy reached out again, and Glad struggled desperately to pull herself up out of the water, onto the edge. Muffy grabbed Glad's legs with both hands, pulled hard, and spat out, "Come down here," between clenched teeth.

Glad felt herself slipping, losing balance, losing control. Her body was rigid with fear; she was being pushed under the water. There was nothing solid under her feet, nothing but water—deep, insubstantial water—and her head was being pushed down under the water. She gasped, and struggled, and gave up as her head went under.

A second later she bobbed up again, gasping and spitting.

Muffy was laughing, treading water.

"You're really terrified of a ducking, aren't you?"

she gloated. "I was only playing. I mean, you professors play with us all the time."

"I'm sorry," said Glad. "I want to get out now."

"Who's stopping you?"

Glad struggled out of the water, and sat, exhausted, panting, on a spectators' bench.

Muffy lay on her back in the water. She floated gracefully. A continuous flow of tears ran down her temples into the sparkling water.

"Muffy?" asked Glad wearily. "You didn't kill him, did you?"

Muffy snuffled, and rolled over in the water, and came out. She shook herself, grabbed a towel, and sat down on the bench, several feet away from Glad.

"No," she said. "But I unlocked the pool for him. I asked him to meet me here, so I could tell him about C.C. and Jack. He came at twelve-thirty, just like he promised; I told him. I told him Jack had made a pass at me, too. I told him I hadn't done anything, and you know what?"

"What?"

"That son-of-a-bitch refused to believe me. Like, he accused me of being like all the others. I mean, Mr. Knight accused me of inviting him here because I wanted him. Wanted the *president!*"

"Didn't you, in a way? I mean, why ask him here at night?"

Muffy paused a moment. "You know, Professor Gold, I mean in a pure way, of course I guess I did. I thought he was like me. I guess I thought he'd admire me for reporting them."

"But he didn't. He humiliated you. You were very angry, weren't you?"

"Yeah. Well, more disappointed, really."

"So then what?"

"So I left. Left him standing down there, at the shallow end. I changed back into my clothes. . . ."

"You were in a bathing suit?"

"Of course. So, you know, if anybody saw me here they'd know I was just practicing."

Glad shook her head. Amazing.

"Yeah. Okay. So you changed, and left, and went back to the dorm?"

"That's right. And then the next day, when he was found, like, I got real scared, you know. I mean, it's totally a relief to tell you this. I've been, like, scared."

"But not too scared to write other anonymous notes."

"Well . . . since Knight was dead, I thought maybe Jack and C.C. would get away with everything after all. . . ."

Glad shook her head. "Muffy, I want you to do something for me."

"Sure," said Muffy apathetically.

"Will you go talk to Dr. Fassett?"

"The shrink?"

"Yes. She's good."

"Whatever for?"

"Just do it for me, okay? You can tell her everything. She won't tell."

Muffy sighed. "Okay."

There were sounds in the spectators' lobby, and Alden Chase walked briskly into the room. "Here you are," he said brightly.

Glad ran to him and fell into his arms. "Oh, Chief, where have you been?" she wailed.

"Looking for you," he said. "I'm glad to see you're in good shape."

"Ha!" she exclaimed.

"Get dressed, honey. We've got to find Mary Anne Reilly."

She looked at him, surprised. "Mary Anne?"

"Yeah. Hurry."

Puzzled, she headed toward the dressing room. Muffy, bouncing again, followed her.

Suddenly, Glad turned, and looked back at the chief with horror.

"Yeah," he said. "I figured out who it is."

"Me, too," she exclaimed, and ran into the dressing room.

Chapter Fifteen

March 18: 9:05 p.m.

MARY ANNE REILLY and Olympia Principe had left the president's dining room together. Glad and the students had already gone; Winston Wulff was giving Mrs. England a lift over to the guest house; Bill Schuster and Palmer Jordan were lingering in the door, saying good-night. The two faculty women, both carrying briefcases, trudged down the path toward the other end of the small campus.

"I have a harmony class to prepare for tomorrow," said Olympia, as they stopped in front of Kola, the music and art building.

"Can't you do it at home?" asked Mary Anne, sympathetically.

Olympia shook her head. "I really need to use the piano, and it wakes my kids if I play at night."

"Well, don't stay up too late."

"I won't. Good-night, Mary Anne. Good luck with your stars."

"Good-night, Olympia."

Olympia took her Kola key out of her pocketbook, unlocked the heavy door, and switched on a light in the lobby. Mary Anne continued on alone. Before she could go to the observatory, she had to stop in her office, in the Goodman building across from Kola. A light was on in Goodman, and the door was unlocked. The guard must be making his rounds.

She ran into him, coming out of the big science auditorium.

" 'Evening, Miss Reilly," he said politely.

" 'Evening, Mr. Emerson."

"Nice night."

"Yes," she said enthusiastically. "Nice and clear."

"Going to be in your office long?"

"Not too long. Maybe a half hour. I'll turn out the lights."

"Okie-dokie, Miss Reilly. Take it easy."

"You, too, Mr. Emerson."

He went on with his rounds. Mary Anne moved along down the hall, past rows of dark, empty labs, to her office across from the botany greenhouse. The faint lavender glow of light from the greenhouse is rather attractive at night, she thought. Wonder if it's time for the night-blooming Cereus again.

Can't be. The botany people would be here, having their earnest little annual Cereus party, with doughnuts and cider.

Not as good as my last eclipse party by a long shot, thought Mary Anne smugly. That eclipse really did a lot for astronomy enrollments.

The event had climaxed at 2 a.m., so Mary Anne and Glad and Howard and Barbara Disher had organized a bash, starting at midnight with wine and cheese. Glad had looked up eclipses in *The Golden Bough*, and had arranged some primitive ceremonies for bringing back the moon. About fifteen faculty and twenty-five students, half-drunk, had solemnly buried some fire (a butane lighter) in the ground outside the observatory, and when the phenomenon was nearing totality, the whole gang had danced around the building, shouting, shaking a tambourine of little Howie Disher's, and throwing sticks and pebbles to scare away the black monster that was eating the moon. Then they had all clattered up the rickety iron stairs to the big telescope—Mary Anne had been a trifle nervous about those old stairs and that noisy troop of revelers. There they had observed the awesome effect of the earth's umbra.

"You look so happy, Mary Anne!" Barbara Disher had said.

Glad had stage-whispered, "She thinks *she's* the one who made it happen. These scientists are always taking credit for the wonders of nature."

That *had* been a happy night. Mary Anne smiled in reminiscence as she put a pot of water to boil on her hot plate. She got two aspirin out of her desk—the sciatica was bad tonight—and went to the drinking fountain in the hall to take them.

She made herself a cup of tea, and got out her observation notebook, and her elaborate charts of the relative positions of double stars. A couple of pairs were really paying off; she was almost sure, now, that she could claim a gravitational effect from unobserved planets. But it would take a long time—perhaps forever—with Turnbull's aged telescope, and New England's cloudy climate. Too long, much too long. In Arizona, it would be a different story. Time was so precious.

Wearily, Mary Anne packed up her briefcase. On one side of the divider were her search committee folders—well, *that* was almost over, thank the Lord—and on the other, her astronomy papers. The briefcase was heavy. Really, too heavy for an aging maiden lady with a ruptured disc. Aging gracefully, mind you. Still somewhat pretty. But, to let Palmer Jordan help her—slippery, reactionary old buzzard—that would have been demeaning.

She turned off the office light, walked back down the corridor, turned off the corridor lights, locked the door of Goodman, and headed for the observatory.

It was a wonderfully clear night; the stars almost blazed at Mary Anne. A clear invitation. She hurried.

Silly Muffy Work. How could Mary Anne be afraid

of the dark? She was an astronomer; the night was her ally, her colleague.

She neared the observatory's big shadow and looked eagerly up at the telescope tower.

A little flicker in the tower window—brief, then no more. A match?

Some funny optical illusion.

The observatory was pretty old; the front door lock hadn't worked well for some time, and Mary Anne had been meaning to get Buildings and Grounds to fix it. Now, it was finally and obviously broken. Before she even turned her key in the lock, Mary Anne felt the door giving; it swung open in an instant.

Mary Anne turned on the downstairs light, and heard a noise.

Creaking, over her head, up in the telescope loft.

The little downstairs classroom was neat and empty, just as Mary Anne had left it after the last class there. Nothing was disturbed; the blackboard was still covered with numbers she had written.

Another creak.

Footsteps?

Still carrying her old leather briefcase, Mary Anne went to the foot of the old iron staircase and started to climb the rickety spiral, watching her feet as she always did on the shaky, narrow steps. The steps seemed to be vibrating more than usual. Alarmed, Mary Anne looked up from the lit downstairs classroom to the dark loft, and saw a big, indistinct shape—a human shape, lifting something large.

The heavy film-holder came hurtling down on her, striking her shoulder, knocking her backward down the steps.

Not my poor *back!* she thought as she staggered and fell, hitting her head on the iron post at the bottom of the staircase.

She was unconscious when Chase, Glad and the security guard found her some time later. The battered film-holder lay on top of her. There wasn't much blood, but papers from her briefcase were scattered all around her at the base of the stairs.

"Call an ambulance right away," said Chase to Emerson. Emerson nodded. "Glad, stay with her; I'll see you at the hospital later. I've got to hurry."

"No," said Glad, agitated. "Don't go alone. Mr. Emerson can take care of Mary Anne; I'm coming with you."

"Okay," he said breathlessly, as they rushed out the door of the observatory. "But I'm going to run."

Glad panted as she struggled to keep up with him, but her long legs helped, and she was able to gasp, as she ran, "The—mu—huh sic—huh building?"

He nodded grimly, and they sprinted in silence.

They were in front of Kola in a minute or two. All seemed quiet. There were lights on in the lobby and one basement room, but the building was eerily still.

They stood in the lobby for a moment, breathing hard.

"Maybe we were wrong?" whispered Chase.

Glad shook her head. "The practice rooms are soundproof. It's this way."

She led him down the stairs, tiptoeing. When they arrived at the basement level, Glad grabbed Chase's arm. At the same time, they both saw the same thing: at the end of the dim hall, outside Olympia's favorite practice room, was someone in a coat, half-crouched, waiting.

Chase looked at Glad, put a silencing finger on his lips, and warned her, with his hand, to stay where she was. Ever so softly, he crept toward the dark figure. When he was almost halfway down the hall, the shape suddenly heard him and turned. He ran full speed at the shape and tackled it just before it got a chance to bash him with the heavy portable telescope. The body came crashing down. Efficiently, Chase pinned it—her—to the floor. Glad half ran toward them.

The practice room door opened, and Olympia looked out of the brightly lit room into the dark hall.

"Glad!" she said, amazed. "What is that man doing sitting on Mrs. England?"

Chapter Sixteen

March 20: 8:40 p.m.

ANOTHER PARTY on Forsythe Street.

"Hey, Howard," asked Olympia, who was a bit tight, "wasn't yesterday Terry's birthday? Did you and Barb tell her any jokes?"

Barbara Disher, looking unusually cuddly in a pink angora sweater, laughed and said, "Yep, we did; it was a roaring success, too. The minister's honeymoon went over very well."

"After Barb explained the punch line to her," Howard pointed out.

Father Bob's handsome face was flushed with embarrassment. "Oh my," he said, "that came from me, didn't it?"

"Right," said Glad.

"I didn't know it was going to be told to a twelve-year-old," protested Bob.

Dean Longfellow heartily slapped the chaplain on the back. "Your sins are forgiven, my son," he said in his booming voice. "What joke did the kid like best?"

"The child psychiatrist one," said Barbara. "We got it from Mandy."

"Wow," said Mandy, "I'm honored."

"Tell it, Mandy," urged Alden Chase.

"Okay. There's this group therapy, you know, three mothers and three kids, and the shrink says to the first mother, 'Madam, it is time for me to tell you what your problem is. You are a miser; you think too much about money—anal, you know?—and the proof of this is that you named your daughter Penny.' "

Bruce Longfellow was chuckling already.

"So," continued Mandy, "he says to the second mother, 'Madam, you are, like, too oral; you think only about food, and the proof of this is that you named your kid Candy.' "

"I can see it coming; I can see it coming!" said Olympia.

"Shut up," said Mandy. "So the third mother grabs her kid by the hand, and before the shrink can speak she says, 'Come on, Dick, we're getting out of here.' "

"Perfect for a twelve-year-old." Barbara Disher smiled.

"Can I get anyone another drink?" asked her husband, ever the perfect host.

"I'll have some more of that scotch," said Alden Chase, untwining his arm from Glad's waist and handing over his empty glass.

"So, Alden," said Mandy insistently, "how did you figure out about Lucille England?"

Chase looked modest. "Routine police procedure," he said. "One of our patrolmen gave a parking ticket to a Rhode Island rent-a-car the night of the murder. We traced the car to the Providence airport. Another rented car—also from the airport—was on Main Street the night Glad's house was burglarized. I knew Mrs. England was supposed to have flown back to Virginia the night of the murder, but she might have waited till her trustee escort left, and then walked back off the plane to the car rental agency. Also, I began to think about Mrs. Pepper and why she left town so fast—she knew that something she had typed could be the most important clue for us."

Mandy spoke up: "But wait a minute, Chiefy. She split also because somebody tried to murder her in the pool. At least, I mean, that's what she told Melanie."

"Oh yes. That, too," admitted Alden. "I heard about that stuff when Mrs. Knight called me. It really puzzled me very much; because of it I kept thinking that the murderer was a man. And one who was here on campus on March the sixteenth."

"So, okay," said Mandy. "So, like, who was that?"

"Yeah," said Disher, "who did something sinister to Mrs. Pepper?"

"Well. I am not able to discuss this at this moment. Uh. Or like ever. Um. Only, well, it was an accident, in a way. Mrs. Pepper was in the pool and someone—well, actually a man—saw the lights on. And, well, Mrs. Pepper swims very well, and for a lady her age has apparently really nice-looking legs, when she's in the water. Anyway, he thought she was another person. One he was expecting to see there. Well, I think I could actually tell you that it was a female that he had had an affair with earlier and has stopped having anything to do with him. Well, he thought it would be a fun surprise to turn the lights off. Then he realized when he heard Mrs. Pepper scream that he could be in real trouble. So he decided, rather stupidly, to scare her enough so she'd leave the building. It worked, of course, but it was mean, really. Court dismissed."

"Oh." "Sure." "Oh, sorry." "Oh I see." Nobody asked any more about the "him." Witherspoon's name was not mentioned by a soul. So Alden continued.

"I had Mrs. Pepper's locked desk drawer opened after I got a legal warrant. Then I read everything written by Mr. Knight on his last day. I found out that one of the people he saw was Lucille England; he had known her before. Knowing that he was an upright sort of person, almost a professional moralist—and hearing from Mrs. Pepper that he thought Lucille England was for some reason an "impossible" candidate—I began to wonder if he had known something about her that would keep her from becoming the next president if he blabbed."

Glad inhaled her cigarette, and added, "That's where I come in."

"How so?" asked Howard. "Did you find out some dirt about England?"

"Well, no, not really," said Glad, "but England was apparently afraid I had. One of her friends at Stott College must have told her that our committee was making inquiries into her background—she mentioned that she knew that at the final dinner— and so she panicked, flew up to Providence the night before the dinner and broke into my house. She took some of my cruddy jewelry to make it look like burglary, but she ditched that under a bush. The only thing really disturbed was my briefcase. When she didn't find anything incriminating in my house, she apparently decided that Mary Anne or Olympia must have been given the grad school detail. So I guess she drove back to the airport, spent the night in a motel, and let herself be picked up the next day by Palmer Jordan and brought here again for her big dinner. She didn't want to kill Mary Anne at the observatory; she just wanted to search her briefcase, but she overdid the knocking-her-out business a bit."

"By the way, how is Mary Anne?" asked Bruce Longfellow, a concerned look on his big red face.

"Fine," said Glad, exhaling. "She'll be back next week. The fall, if anything, did some kind of mysterious good thing for her back—maybe jiggled the pieces of ruptured disc away from the sciatic nerve or something. Does that make sense?"

"Yeah," said Bruce, "I've heard of cures like that."

"Anyway, she's got a headache, but her back pain is less than it's been for years. And she's grouchy as hell about the broken film-holder."

Bruce chuckled. "Maybe she'll be less sore when

she finds out that Mrs. Day and I have agreed she needs to go to Kitt Peak for a year."

"Mrs. Day?" asked Mandy excitedly.

"Oops," said Bruce.

"Shut up," said Glad.

"Oh, well," said Olympia. "It'll be announced next week anyway. Diane Day has agreed to be our new president."

"But please keep it quiet," said Glad, "till the final trustee confirmation."

"How totally great!" exploded Mandy. "Will she be as with it as she seems?"

"Who knows?" replied Glad. "It's a tough time for colleges generally, and a particularly tough time for the raft of women presidents who have come in for the first time. In the sixties, college presidents could do no wrong. No matter what they did, their schools flourished. Now—well. Anyhow, Day has already handed down solid opinions on several issues. For one thing, she's decided that all faculty members finishing up terminal contracts this year should be given another year's contract, and a re-examination of their status next year when she can take part in it."

"Wait a minute!" said Howard, almost spilling his beer. "How many of those are there?"

"I can only think of one," said Glad, smiling.

"Oh, Howard," cried Barbara Disher, jumping up and hugging him.

"Anything else?" asked Mandy. "Like, is she going to have a lover in the president's house?"

Glad smiled. "Alas, no. Sorry, Mandy. But since she doesn't have a president's wife to run parties for her, the trustees have agreed to let her have a live-in social secretary. Guess who?"

"Melanie Knight?" asked Barbara Disher tentatively.

Glad nodded.

"Perfect," said Mandy, and the others agreed.

"Now, I mean, Glad, and, uh, Alden, we need to know more about, you know, England. What was her secret, and what happened the night of the murder?"

Chase looked inquiringly at Glad. "You want to tell it, Doctor?" he asked.

"Okay, Chief," she said. "I'll tell about the secret; you tell about the murder."

"Okay," he said, and took a sip of his drink.

"Her secret," said Glad, "was that she had no Ph.D. It wasn't a thesis problem—she did do that, and even made it into a good book, apparently, but she was never able to pass the language exam, which all candidates had to do before being allowed to write dissertations. Dotty old Professor Hinnerschütz was right: she had a problem with German. As I've found out since, she flunked the foreign language exam once, and her adviser, who thought the language requirement was silly for American historians, let her start work on the thesis anyway, figuring she'd pass it the next time. Well, she tried twice more, and failed both times. By then, she'd almost finished her thesis, had a contract with a publisher, and an instructorship at Stott College. So she left Berkeley, told Stott she *had* the degree, got her thesis published, and no one ever knew."

"My God," said Mandy.

Chase shook his head. "It still surprises me," he said, "to think that she didn't get found out earlier. Don't they ask to see your diploma when you get a job?"

Glad laughed. "Most places figure that would be insulting, I think. Were you ever asked for proof of your degree, Howard?"

Howard shook his head. Olympia added, "Neither was I. We're all honorable persons."

"All right," said Mandy. "So how does Knight fit into all this?"

"Well," said Glad, "apparently he was a young assistant professor when Lucille was in grad school, and he knew all about her debacle with German. But she left and went to Virginia, and he ended up here. Our dear departed hadn't thought about her since then. He probably figured she had transferred to another university which didn't have a language requirement—that's done sometimes. So then she shows up as a candidate for his job, with a vita that clearly says Ph.D., Berkeley, 1960. And he informs her, in his interview with her, that he's a man of principle and is going to tell all. You take it from here, Chief."

Chase took a breath. "Okay," he said. "So she goes away from her interview mighty worried, because she's insanely ambitious, and it looks as if she's got a good chance of getting this job. After dinner, Jane Della Rosa drives her to the airport, and at some point, sooner or later, Lucille decides to come back to Wading River secretly, to try to persuade Knight to keep his mouth shut. She figures, after all, she'd be a responsible president. Isn't all her administrative experience more important than a silly language exam?"

"Like wow," said Mandy.

"Go on," urged Bruce Longfellow.

"Okay," said the chief. "So she comes back to Wading River and parks her rented car on Main Street, then walks over to the president's house. By now it's well after eleven o'clock at night. But she doesn't want to be seen by any of the search committee, who all think she's on a plane headed for Virginia, and she sees a bunch of faculty lushes coming out of a house on Forsythe. . . ."

"That's us!" exclaimed Barbara Disher.

Chase nodded. "So she hides in the president's side garden, and maybe peeks in the window to see if he's alone."

"But he wasn't alone," added Glad. "He and Melanie were together in the study until she went to bed, shortly after midnight. Lucille must have gotten pretty discouraged and chilly waiting in the bushes."

"Yeah," said Chase, "but the prize was worth waiting for. Anyway, Mrs. Knight goes to bed, and Mrs. England is just about to knock on the window, when the rowdy faculty drunks come staggering out of the pool, shouting 'good-night' and 'ad astra per aspera' and stuff like that at each other."

"That couldn't have been us," said Mandy, shaking her head. "I mean, I never say good-night. I always say something like 'take care.' And Howard says, 'See you later, alligator.' "

"Stow it, Mandy," said the dean to the Dean of Students. "So Lucille keeps hiding in the bushes?"

"Yeah," said Chase. "And in the meantime the witching hour has struck, and Patrolman Heuser has given her car a ticket and noted the license plate. Now Lucille sees another interesting thing. Melanie has gone to bed and Knight has put on his coat. He is coming out the side door and walking quickly through his garden, right past Lucille, through the gate and over to the pool. Lucille follows at a discreet distance. Then, she sees that someone is waiting for Knight at the pool door, a student with curly blond hair. They enter the building, leaving the door unlocked. Lucille enters, too, unnoticed by them, and waits in the spectators' lobby while they have a brief and unpleasant conversation. The student leaves. Knight remains, thoughtfully staring at the expensive pool he conned old Mrs. Pearce into underwriting."

"Did Mrs. England tell you all this?" asked Bruce Longfellow. "Or are you conjecturing?"

"I'm guessing some of it," said the Chief, running a hand through his fair, straight hair, "but she's confirmed all the important details. She says she didn't plan to kill him. She only tried to plead with him to keep quiet on the grounds that her offense was so trivial and so long ago."

"I don't think it was trivial," said Olympia.

"Neither did Knight," said Chase. "He gave her a stern lecture about honor and duty and propriety, and in a moment of what the lady has wisely decided to call insanity, she grabbed a handy baseball bat, bashed his handsome silver head, and pushed him into the pool. She drove back to the airport, returning the car at one forty-eight a.m., and sensibly paying for it with cash, took the next plane to somewhere farther south, and began worrying a lot."

"Not very good judgment," commented Olympia. "If she had just withdrawn from candidacy, she'd never have been found out, would she?"

"Probably not," said Chase.

"And nobody," said Glad, "except Professor Hinnerschütz would ever have known she couldn't read German."

"But she wanted to be president of a college so much," said Longfellow sadly.

"Crazy," said Mandy Tweedy. "Like *totally* crazy."